No woman could love the Dom he'd become.

Luc Christianson can't live through the anguish of losing another woman he loves. For a few moments of carnal release at Bacchus House, Niagara's members-only BDSM club, he escapes the constant ache of loss. But he has two firm rules — never play with the same sub twice, and emotions are never part of the scene.

Submission can only begin when she learns to trust herself.

Journalist Avery Lewis is putting her life back together after she escapes her abusive husband. He never grasped safe, sane, and consensual. She's earning back what he stole from her — career, self-esteem, and the ability to trust. But there's a piece missing. Avery's a submissive despite the fact her body jumps into full flight mode when she begins to relinquish control.

A chance meeting at a wine tasting event reignites an undeniable connection Luc and Avery shared in high school, but never acted upon. She craves Luc's brand of Dominance and revels in the boundless pleasure he extracts from her body. He needs to watch her flourish under his hand, to move beyond her past and fully embrace her submission to him. Only him.

But sometimes, the place you feel safest is where your worst nightmare comes to life.

When Avery receives a series of sinister messages Luc's

protective instincts roar to life. But Avery refuses to let any man, or her past, control her life.

Show Me How to Live: Part 1 is a blistering hot novel with plenty of suspense to keep you guessing. Luc and Avery's HEA comes in *Show Me How to Live: Part 2*, but not without a shocking twist that will leave you breathless.

If you enjoy sexy romance with a healthy dollop of suspense, like Roni Loren, Lexi Blake, and Cherise Sinclair, the *Show Me How to Live* duet will leave you hot and satisfied.

SHOW ME HOW TO LIVE: PART 1

A BACCHUS HOUSE NOVEL (BOOK 1)

HÉLÈNE SOPER

Show Me How to Live: Part 1

Edited by Judy Roth
Cover Design by Clarity Book Cover Design
Ebook Design by MarksEbookFormatting.com

First edition: December 2018
HeleneSoper.com

DEDICATION

To abuse survivors, men and women, and their children who through sheer resilience demonstrate immeasurable courage by living their own lives.

Fifty cents from the sale of this book, and Show Me How to Live Part 2, will be donated to Gillian's Place.

As one of Ontario's first shelters for abused women and children, Gillian's Place has been providing safe refuge and non-residential programs that enable women and their children to break the cycle of violence for over 40 years. www.Gilliansplace.com

CONTENTS

The room was an assault on the senses. Mouth-watering aromas drifted from the chefs' stations dotting the center of the Fallsview Casino's main ballroom. Opulent floral arrangements were strategically placed to frame regional vignettes — Niagara-on-the-Lake wineries clustered in one area, Prince Edward County wineries took up residence in another. Proud winemakers and winery owners were on hand to personally pour their top vintages for select members of the media and enthusiastic consumers who were prepared to pay the hefty price for a ticket. Clinking glasses punctuated the echoes of laughter and backslapping.

Luc adjusted the sharply creased cuffs of his tuxedo jacket and fingered his cuff links as he surveyed every inch of the room. Everything was perfect. The Ontario Vintner's Awards, the wine industry's annual awards gala, was Luc Christianson's debut as Sky Hill Estate Winery's president. Winning the prestigious "Red Wine of the Year" at the award ceremony earlier in the evening had been an unexpected surprise and the ideal opportunity for his dad, Billy, to announce his retirement and Luc as his successor. Now every reporter and wine blogger in the room wanted a piece of him.

The move home promised to propel Luc toward something positive — taking the helm of Sky Hill Estate Winery, his family's business in Niagara-on-the-Lake. This was always the plan, from the day Luc entered law school he knew he would follow his roots home, eventually. Tragedy had simply expedited the timing. He hoped he wouldn't have to rehash the sorrow of losing the most important women in his life — which he'd successfully buried — just to feed a reporter's lust for salacious details. Death, no matter how long ago, seemed to be always newsworthy. Luc steeled his spine as he plastered on his best wine-guy smile to face the scrum.

"Luc, you've made a name for yourself as a corporate lawyer in Toronto, made partner in a Bay Street firm, why give that up to come home to Niagara to helm your family's winery?"

Luc had spent the past few weeks since his move from Toronto getting up to speed on not only Sky Hill's business but also the trends and issues in the industry. He was ready for any question a reporter might throw his way. This softball question was no reason to let his guard down. Reporters could be every bit the shark his former courtroom opponents were.

"Thanks for asking, Mike. It's simple. It was time. My roots are here, pardon the pun. Even though my law practice had me based in Toronto, Niagara was never far from my heart. I've been helping out behind the scenes for years. Dad feels it's time for him to reduce his workload, travel a bit, not stress about the day-to-day operations. My job will be to honor the foundation my parents built with Sky Hill back when no one believed we could grow world-class wine grapes here in Niagara. He proved them wrong in fine fashion. Now we need to take the company into the future and capitalize on the growing demand for Canadian wine."

What Luc didn't say was the winery gave him purpose again because the law sure didn't fire him up like it used to. Sky Hill represented a future he could embrace, even though that future looked markedly different than it once did. As president of his family's business he'd be responsible for the livelihood of more than fifty employees and their families. No longer could Luc stand back and watch as the world was spun on its axis, unable or unwilling to engage with the people around him. An automaton going through the motions of life without feeling the all-consuming pain of his loss. He needed to step up, put the past behind him, and get down to business to ensure Sky Hill had a rosy future.

"I won't be doing this alone." Luc reached behind him to bring his middle sister to the front of the scrum. "I'd like to introduce you to my sister, Geneviève. She's been working in New Zealand for the past few years after graduating from U.C. Davis with her master's in Viticulture and Oenology. Dad and I are thrilled she's bringing her knowledge and expertise to Sky Hill. We want her making our wines, not our competitors'. And our youngest sister, Anne-Sophie, is also here this evening. She's taking the official photos tonight so be sure to have your game face on."

Everyone in their circle chuckled right on cue.

A tingling awareness washed over his skin as he shook a reporter's hand. He glanced over the man's shoulder toward the ballroom doors. His heart stopped.

God, she was gorgeous. Her blonde hair was swept up at the back as a few loose tendrils accentuated her elegant neck. Her lavender gown skimmed decadent curves. Beads formed a flower that nestled perfectly below her breasts while its stem pointed his eyes to a slit that exposed a sinfully sexy amount of leg. His arousal grew just looking at her.

Hold on.

Was that his high school English tutor, Avery Lewis?

Detective Gryffin Calder, Luc's best friend since grade school, had mentioned yesterday when they met for their weekly sparring workout that he was Avery's plus-one for the evening.

But. Holy. Shit.

Gryff gave him the bro nod with his chin. Luc nodded back. He hadn't seen Avery for years. Back in high school, Luc had thought she was sweet, pretty, and was much too innocent for his dark desires. His body reacted to her now as it had back then — he couldn't take his eyes off her and his dick strained to get closer. But now she was a sexy-as-hell woman. A winemaker stepped in front of Avery to kiss her on both cheeks. She gave a professional smile and kissed him back then followed him to a table and disappeared from Luc's view.

Someone cleared their throat, bringing Luc's attention back to the group huddled near his family. He stuck out his hand to shake the one in front of him, though he couldn't have cared less who was attached to the other end. His brain was focused entirely on catching another glimpse of her. He heard his father saying something, but it was as if he were underwater, hearing the sounds but not discerning the words.

Gen shoved her elbow into Luc's ribs, dissipating the fog in his head.

"What's got your undivided attention big brother?"

"Nothing." Luc tried to even out his breathing, but Avery came back into view and he hoped like hell no one heard his grade-school gasp.

"I call bullshit." Gen followed his line of sight. "Wow, she's hot. Wait. Is that Avery Lewis?"

Luc made his way across the room, ignoring his sister. Light and sound faded away, every nerve fiber was attuned to Avery's presence. He couldn't take his eyes off her. Oh, what he wanted to do with that spectacular ass. Visions of her porcelain skin, red from his hand, made his dick harder than the steel posts he spent summers pounding into the ground at the end of each vineyard row. He couldn't remember the last time he'd had such a visceral reaction to a woman. But she wasn't just a random woman. She was no longer the girl who listened to his lame-ass stories about the locker room pranks perpetrated by his football teammates. The girl who spent as much time learning about AC/DC, Queen, and Led Zeppelin from him as he had learned about Shakespeare and the great American novel from her.

Avery sampled some wines and chatted with the winemaker. She exuded poise and confidence as she mingled with the wine pros. Fuck that was sexy. Gryff and Avery appeared quite comfortable with each other, touching each other with familiarity accorded to very good friends, or lovers. But, Gryff said they were just friends.

What the hell was he thinking? Luc had never been the jealous type, and he had no claim on Avery.

Luc shook his head at where his mind was going. These past five years were governed by one unbreakable rule — play with a sub once. Sex was sex. Scenes were transactional, negotiated, fulfilled then forgotten. Feelings were never part of the mix. But Avery wasn't a club sub he could scene with and forget. He needed to get his control back in check and move on. An ache constricted his chest. Breathing normally became wishful thinking. Guilt anchored his feet to the floor as he desperately tried to will the throbbing in his cock to calm the fuck down. Avery could never be his. Why did that notion feel like a kick in the gut?

"This is our twenty-fifteen Pinot Noir grown on our estate vineyard. It was all hand-harvested and spent twelve months in one-year-old French oak."

"Well, Frank, I think you have a winner here. I love the spicy notes on the finish. The red fruit is bright and fresh. Nicely balanced."

Avery liked the wine well enough but knew from previous tastings it wouldn't be her favorite in the room. As she emptied the remainder of her glass into the spittoon she felt a presence behind her — a warm, sensual awareness that set her skin aflame.

"Hey man, congrats on the award." Avery vaguely heard Gryff say to someone as he reached out to bump fists.

"Thanks. It was a good opportunity to announce the changes at Sky Hill. So far, the reaction has been positive."

God, that voice. She'd recognize it anywhere. And his scent — a heady aroma of pure male musk mingled with a warm spice that was uniquely Luc Christianson. It enveloped her in a cozy, pheromone-laden cloak that seeped into her bones, filling spaces she didn't know were empty. She couldn't control the shudder that racked her body from head to toe. Heat climbed up her neck, flushed her cheeks, and sent a rush of dampness between her thighs. She took in a deep breath and slowly faced him.

Her logical brain flew the coop leaving her body, which had its own agenda, in charge. He looked as delicious as he smelled — warm spice like a good Pinot Noir, layered with his unique musk. His thick chestnut hair had grown out since she last saw him a couple of years ago at his mother's funeral. Imagining running her fingers through the glossy waves made her knees weak and her sex throb.

Just like back in high school, her body had an instinctual reaction to the mere presence of this man. Quarterback of the senior football team, lead guitarist in the rock band that played their weekend dances, the super-hot guy all the girls wished they could call their boyfriend. Avery's teenage crush was standing right there. Looking at her. His eyes feasting on her. And her body responded like Pavlov's dogs.

"How's your dad handling the change in his routine? Is he dialing back a bit?" Gryff asked.

Luc chuckled. The low rumble set off a cascade of answering vibrations in parts of her body she hadn't heard from in years. Luc's eyes released their hold on her as he answered their friend's question. Finally, her lungs expanded, taking in much needed oxygen.

"Come on, Gryff, you know he won't altogether retire from this way of life, but he's stoked about getting away for a bit of downtime. He's been going nonstop since Mom died. He needs a break."

Luc's focus swiveled back onto Avery as he extended his hand. She hesitated for a brief second and glanced up at his gorgeous face, mesmerized by his warm, molten brown eyes. He had always been an old soul, sharing a world of experience and depth of emotion in a simple glance. For a heartbeat, a stark emptiness shrouded the life in his gaze but in a blink, it was gone to be replaced by the trademarked, panty-melting, Christianson dimpled smirk. She practically jumped out of her skin when Gryff grazed her arm. It was probably too much to ask that no one noticed.

"Avery," Gryff said, "you remember Luc from high school."

She placed her hand in the one Luc courteously offered and managed to nod. Her tongue was rendered useless, plastered against the roof of her mouth. Luc's eyes got darker, the pupils dilating, all but crowding out the irises. She was floored by the surging hunger in his eyes. And all his masculine energy was directed at her. This was her longest running fantasy coming to life. Her heartbeat accelerated like a thoroughbred breaking out of the starting gate. She hoped he didn't feel the trembling telegraphing down her arm she was desperately trying to control.

All bets were off when he leaned in and planted a friendly kiss on each cheek. A lovely custom practiced throughout Wine Country, one in which she participated in regularly with friends and colleagues. But none ignited the possibilities of "what if" as this one from Luc. He seemed to linger for a moment as if taking in her scent, his breath causing goose bumps to erupt across her skin.

Who was she kidding? Luc could have any gorgeous woman in the room with nothing more than a wolfish smile and a few skillfully chosen words. She was the girl who tutored him in English. The buddy who he used as a sounding board devising plans on how to get into the pants of his latest fling. Nothing more.

Avery needed to get her head out of the past and remember she was here to do a job. She pulled away from the envelope of masculine heat that seeped into her bones. A chill crawled up her arm as he dropped her hand, severing their connection, allowing the cooler air of the room to glide over her sensitized skin.

Turning to his side, Luc extended his elbow. "May I? I'd love to get your opinion on our wines."

Avery tucked her hand into the crook of his arm so he could escort her to the Sky Hill table. Each point of contact — hand, arm, hip — was set aflame by his touch. His innate sexuality smoldered, barely concealed by his tux. She was on the arm of the sexiest guy in the room. Eyes followed them as they made their way across the floor. When did walking become a mind-bending proposition?

"Gen, you remember Avery Lewis."

"I sure do. I love your dress, Avery. May I pour you a glass of wine?"

"Thanks, Gen. You look great. I'd love a glass. I understand you're planning on taking over the winemaking duties from your father."

"Give her the Estate Bottled Chardonnay," Luc said. "And yes, we can't wait to have her home for good once she finishes up the harvest in New Zealand."

Gen poured the wine and handed the glass to Luc who took it by the stem. His elegant long fingers cradled the delicate crystal with such reverence Avery mused what they would feel like tracing patterns on her skin. Would his hands be soft or calloused? Would he be gentle or demanding? Would his fingers or tongue get her hot faster?

She held out her hand, her gaze never leaving his, as he handed her the glass. Sizzling electricity wound its way up her arm from where his fingers brushed hers. A patented Luc half-smile curled his lips. And it was directed at her. That was enough to make the dampness between her legs feel like Niagara Falls and anything she was thinking about vanish into the mist.

Gryff's phone buzzed, breaking her delicious spell. A grim look overtook her friend's face when he read the text.

"Sorry, Avery, it's work. I have to go in."

"Is everything OK?"

Avery hoped her voice didn't betray her sudden anxiety at him leaving her at the event before she was able to call it a night. She still had several more producers to interview. She had a job to do and couldn't let stupid, irrational fear get in her way. She was a professional, damn it!

"Yeah. Possible lead on a case we're working." Gryff sighed

and put down his wine glass. "Let me arrange for a cab to take you home when you're ready."

"Don't worry, brother. I've got her. I'll make sure she gets home safe and sound," Luc said as he stepped closer to Avery and put his hand on the small of her back.

Decadent heat radiated outward from his palm, like the sun's rays her eight-year-old daughter, Cassidy, drew in her pictures. The tension in her shoulders eased and the heartbeat that threatened to strangle her esophagus managed to relocate back into her chest.

"Perfect. Thanks man." Gryff turned to Avery and brushed his hand up and down her arm. "I'm sorry I have to leave. But I know you're in good hands with Luc. You don't need to worry about a thing. Enjoy your evening. I'll expect a full report tomorrow. Who knows, the big guy may even give you an exclusive interview." Gryff nodded toward his buddy as he said his good nights and strode with purpose out of the ballroom.

Avery sighed. One day she wouldn't be that woman who still needed to be taken care of by her big bad cop friend. She was a grown woman, a survivor, a professional journalist, not a basket case. Damn it all to hell and back.

"Thanks, Luc, but I'm a big girl. I can take a cab. The newspaper will pay for it since I'm here on official business."

"Like hell I'm letting you take a cab home." Luc's dark eyes bored into her, leaving her a little breathless. "When you're ready, I'll drive you home. It would be my pleasure, Avery."

His alpha male tone made her nipples harden into granite and her clit throb. Why did her body react to Mr. Bossypants like she was some wanton sexpot who would obediently drop to her knees at his feet at the first sign of authority?

Simple. Avery had discovered a long time ago she was a submissive. But that precious gift wasn't cherished or respected by the Dom she'd chosen to help her learn about the lifestyle. Now, Avery equated submission with relinquishing her humanity. And she'd vowed to never dip her toe in that pond again.

But her body didn't get the memo. Luc's deep, authoritative tone quelled her anxiety brought on by Gryff leaving her at the event. Luc's apparent need to make sure she got home safely flipped her sub switch on and into the fully locked position. She yearned for a caring, protective Dom like she'd read about in her smutty novels. Yet, she couldn't risk falling under the spell of another commanding asshole pretending to give a shit about her and her daughter.

She needed to get her head out of her own ass, pronto. Luc wasn't commanding her to strip and present. It was just a ride home. Once she was safely ensconced in her own bedroom, she could use her plug-in magic wand to ease the ache Luc ignited. There she would have control over her body and its reactions, restraints not required.

She took in a deep breath and held her head high. "Fine. Let me do my job then I'll meet you back here. Say, in an hour."

"One hour. I'll be here."

Avery strolled to the next table on her mental list. No matter where she went or how many wines she tasted over the next sixty minutes, she felt Luc's laser-like glare heating up her backside with every step she took. Shit, she was more annoyed with her recalcitrant body for answering his carnal draw than she was with the man himself. She used every minute away from him to attempt to clear his voice, his touch, his scent out of her brain so she could get a ride home from the sexiest guy she'd ever known without bowing her head and calling him "Sir".

No pressure.

2

Sixty minutes felt like an eternity. Luc's gaze was glued to her every move as she worked the room like a pro. She took her time giving each winemaker her full attention. He watched in fascination as she stopped at specific tables and deftly evaluated each sample — gentle swirl of the glass, glass to nose, deep inhale, glass to lips, swish sample to coat mouth, then spit or swallow. She shined as brilliantly as the harvest moon rising in the night sky.

Since when did the process of critically evaluating a wine become a sensual act? He'd seen people swirl and suck wine his entire life — hell, he'd done it thousands of times. Yet, no one else made his cock stand at attention the way she did when she swirled and sucked. And how she used just her fingertips to hold the stem of the glass evoked visions of those slender fingers stroking his shaft. His erection strained against his zipper to the point of pain. Thank God his tux jacket covered his crotch. He slipped his hand into his pocket while he stood behind the Sky Hill table trying to adjust himself to a more comfortable position.

Not a chance. Only one thing would relieve this throbbing. How sweet would her nipples taste as he nipped and sucked? How gorgeous would she look when she flew apart as her pussy milked his shaft buried deep inside her? If he didn't get his mind off her he would explode in his pants right in the middle of the ballroom. Not exactly how he wanted to be remembered by his new colleagues.

A flash of blonde hair in the crowd caught his attention. The hair on the back of his neck stood up. Only one other blonde had elicited that reaction from him, and no way she would have followed him to Niagara. They hadn't exchanged last names when they played at a party before he moved home. And she knew the deal — once and done. He shook off the odd sensation and resumed surveying the room for Avery, the only blonde he wanted in his sightline or imagination. She caught him looking and a sweet crimson hue made its way up her throat to flush her cheeks. He loved to see that color on a woman. Correction. On that woman.

Avery held up her hand, splaying all fingers indicating she would be ready in five minutes. He managed to give her a curt nod, not bad considering every muscle in his body was as taut as a vineyard trellis wire. Anticipation of touching her silky skin and her summer-fresh scent filling his nose sent tendrils of lust through his body, twisting and turning, latching onto any anchor it could find so it could grow toward the source of its sustenance. Her.

Everything about Avery called to Master Luc. The way she reluctantly met his gaze, how the pulse point in her neck throbbed when he kissed her cheeks, how her pert nipples pebbled at the sound of his voice. He'd been a Dom long enough to recognize a sub's response. His curiosity was as aroused as his dick.

Avery had matured into a beautiful, desirable woman, but this wasn't just lust slamming his system. A tentativeness telegraphed from her like a beacon — like she was unaware of how she affected men in her orbit. Fascinating. He certainly saw how masculine eyes, and a few feminine ones, followed her graceful curves as she moved from table to table. Yet, the naïveté he remembered remained. Nothing like the trained submissives he played with who understood their power and knew how to wield it.

Whoever the men were in her past were idiots if she questioned for a second she wasn't a goddess who deserved to be worshiped. Luc wanted, no needed, to be the Dom to peel off those layers of insecurity to reveal her radiant core. Ideas for scenes floated through his mind like a steamy, intense, and wickedly pleasurable movie. Each time negative thoughts or feelings of embarrassment invaded her mind she would earn his punishment. Picturing the mark of his hand on her ass made his cock pulse in time with his heartbeat, the echo hammering inside his chest. A scene or two wouldn't be enough to satisfy this craving.

He'd had only one committed D/s relationship, with Sydney. And they'd learned the ropes together. Since then, he'd negotiated pick-up play with experienced subs on the spot. One sub for one scene. That was it. Somehow, Avery felt different. Guilt slammed him in the gut. Wanting more than a scene with Avery was tantamount to betraying his vows with Sydney. His wife.

Luc sensed Avery's presence before a gentle touch on his elbow signaled her return to his side, completely distracting him from the conversation he was having with a colleague. All the blood in his body coursed straight to his groin but the gaping hole in his heart pounded with the intensity of a bass drum at a rock concert. Luc had become the master of control, cool under pressure, the Master novice Doms and subs turned to for advice. Somehow Avery knocked his control on its ass. It was time to lock down his surging desire and regain control of his wayward head, both big and little.

"I'm ready when you are, Luc. But don't rush on my account."

Her voice drifted over Luc like a gentle summer rain, sparking life into his soul that had been dormant for so long. With a tilt of her head and sweep of her lashes Avery gifted Luc with a smoldering smile that melted the lock on his beast's cage. It wasn't a contrived or deceitful look. It was an honest-to-goodness sweet glance betraying that her quiet reserve was still underneath the professional and friendly demeanor she exuded. How she maintained that modesty from high school he would never know, but it did something for him. In a big way.

"Before we go, can we set up a time this week for me to come by Sky Hill to interview you, Gen, and your dad? I'm working on a piece about generational change in the wine business, and your family would be perfect."

Luc's father responded before Luc could get his voice to cooperate. "Of course, Avery. We'd be delighted to chat with you. I'm heading to our place in Florida in the morning, but I'll make myself available by phone any time this week, whenever you and Luc and Gen find a time that works for you."

"Thank you, Billy. I'm looking forward to it. Have a safe flight and enjoy Florida."

Luc couldn't wait any longer.

"Good night everyone. Time to get Avery home."

He placed his hand at the small of her back to guide her toward the door before his dad and sister could say their farewells. His mom would be disappointed in his lack of manners, but at this moment he didn't give a shit. He ushered them from the room at warp speed.

The tension in Avery's muscles eased as she relaxed against his hand. Such a beautiful response. One that only served to feed his beast.

A very was taken aback by the urgency of Luc's hand pressing at her back, steering her toward the ballroom door. Her strappy heels, which looked spectacular on the store shelf and matched her dress perfectly, were definitely not made for a brisk walk anywhere.

"Slow down a minute, Luc. What's the rush?" Avery slipped her hand between his torso and arm to latch onto his bicep in an attempt to staunch his pace. "Would you mind if I made a quick pit stop into the ladies' room before we hit the road?"

Luc abruptly stopped and blinked several times as he looked down at her. She would have been flat on her ass if she hadn't been holding on to his arm.

"Of course. No problem," Luc said as he shoved his hand through his hair.

"Thank you. I'll just be a minute."

"Take your time. I'll be right here."

Avery ducked into the bathroom to gather her thoughts. She stopped in front of the row of designer sinks artfully attached to the natural-colored engineered stone counters and waved her hands under the chrome faucet to start the flow. Cool water engulfed her hands, snapping her swirling thoughts to a halt. She gave up trying to decipher the words Luc said and the emotions his eyes left unsaid. She had to be reading more into what she thought she saw. Luc was happy to see his old high school friend. That was it.

The sound of a stall opening caught Avery's attention. Over

her shoulder in the mirror a lithe, drop-dead-gorgeous blonde sashayed to the counter. The obvious platinum color-job didn't detract from the woman's star quality sex appeal. Her high cheekbones, plumped crimson lips, and full, high breasts fit with the persona she exuded. She was sexy, and she knew it. And not afraid to wear it like a badge of honor. This was the type of woman she pictured at Luc's side. Confident. Powerful. Seductive. Catching her own image in the mirror Avery sighed and pulled her hands away from the sink to reach for paper towels, fighting the encroaching anxiety heralding a looming panic attack.

No one knew how she fought the gnawing fingers of trepidation from claiming her every time she stepped into public. At the first sign of their usual barrage of twists and pokes in her stomach she would close her eyes, take several deep, cleansing breaths, and start her "leaving the house" checklist, whether she was at home and did it live or visualizing the process wherever she was at the time — bathroom water off, vanity doors closed, counter clean, lights off. Next, she would straighten her duvet cover, line up the pillow stacks the cat, Mr. Chester, invariably had toppled over, put the dress hanger back in the dress section of her closet, and close the door. One last scan of her room would satisfy her inner neat freak sufficiently that everything was in its proper place, so she could leave her house with her sanity relatively intact. At least it would appear that way to anyone who casually observed her. She closed her eyes and in her head ran through one of her checklists.

One more cleansing breath and her heartbeat downshifted back into the normal range. Avery slipped her clutch under her arm, gave herself one last check in the mirror to make sure everything was tucked in and smoothed down. She gave the other woman a polite smile in the mirror before she left and was miffed at the cold stare she received in return. She never under-stood how some women treated every other woman as if she was a competitor to be distained. Avery shook her head and walked out the door. After all, her secret crush was waiting to drive her home. Who was waiting for blondie?

3

L uc peered down a darkened corridor that led toward the ballroom service area. It was empty. He grabbed Avery's hand and pulled her behind him.

"What the hell are you doing?"

She tried to pull her hand free, but Luc squeezed and looked back, capturing her gaze.

"Come with me."

His voice was firm, direct, and an octave lower. She hesitated for a split second, but he saw the moment she stopped her internal battle and gave over to him. Fuck, that was sexy.

Halfway down the darkened corridor, in a spot where a faint glow of light gave way to sultry shadows, he spun her around, took her upper arms in his hands and pressed her back against the wall. Tendrils of light caressed her delicate skin barely revealing her features.

"Oh!"

He slid his hands over her shoulders, up her neck to cup her cheeks, tipping her face up for their eyes to meet. "I've been watching you all night." His voice sounded like he gargled rocks for fun.

"I noticed." Her voice was barely a whisper.

They were nose to nose, breathing in each other's essence. Shallow, rapid breaths told Luc she was either nervous or aroused. Which one?

"I've been dying to find out how your skin would feel under my tongue since the moment you walked into the room tonight. I'll bet you taste like heaven. If you don't want me to touch you, tell me now."

Luc waited a few heartbeats and watched as her pupils swallowed the sky blue of her irises. Bingo. Definitely arousal.

"I…I thought about you, too. I should have been focusing on the wines, but for some reason I was a little distracted."

"Distracted, hmm. What if I feathered my fingertips down the graceful slope of your neck, like this, and continued to trace a line to your beating pulse at the base of your throat? Or how about instead of my fingers I used my tongue to gently trace the path?" He used the tip of his tongue to illustrate his point. "Would that be a distraction?"

"Oh, definitely."

Ravenous with need, fueled by her sighs, his arousal rocketed into the stratosphere. She smelled and tasted divine. As he braced his forearms against the wall on either side of her, Avery's head lolled to the side, exposing her neck for his taking and her eyes fluttered closed.

"Open your eyes, Avery. I need to see your eyes. I need you to see I'm the man who's making you ache to be touched."

"Oh God, Luc."

The spot behind her ear felt as soft as a baby's belly, and just as sensitive, judging from how her breath caught when he nuzzled his nose against it. He continued exploring her elegant neck from jaw to collarbone, marking his favorite spots with a nip of his teeth and a soothing lick. Her heartbeat pulsated in a steady rhythm along her neck and her eyelids threatened to obscure her vision.

"Do you know how fucking sexy you are?"

She brushed her hands around his waist and smoothed her palms up his back. He shivered. Luc rarely allowed subs to touch him. He was able to keep himself apart from them if he controlled the physical connection, usually by binding their hands. But he liked how he felt when Avery touched him and the way her gaze all but devoured him. He was more than a slab of muscle who knew how to deliver an orgasm. She made him feel worthy of her attention. Her touch had awakened feelings he thought were long dead and buried.

"This isn't the time or the place to explore this heat between us. But I can't walk away and not explore you a little."

"Please, Luc."

"Please what, Avery. Tell me what you want, right here, right now."

He floated his palms along the soft skin of her arms, pulled them out from under his suit jacket, pinned them behind her back in one of his hands and gently pressed her shoulders against the wall as he placed his other hand at the base of her neck and lightly closed his fingers around the porcelain column. He closed the gap between his fingers and thumb with a gentle pulse and release to gauge her reaction. Her back arched farther, thrusting her perfect breasts into his chest as her body tensed and her breath caught in her throat on a gasp.

His eyes didn't leave hers. He saw intense desire there, marred by uncertainty. He stilled, waiting for her to decide whether she was on board with his plan. Not that he really had a plan, which was bewildering.

This whole evening was so out of the realm of his usual sexual encounters. Limits weren't discussed. Roles weren't established. Luc was still a Dom down to his last molecule, and he found comfort and purpose in those shoes. But this was different, whatever this was. Luc, the man, was in the driver's seat and he couldn't get enough of the woman in his arms. Master Luc just needed to keep them safely on the road.

It took only a few seconds for Avery's body to relax and mold into his. Luc took his time cataloging every signal her body put out. Her responsiveness pulled the Master out of the back seat and placed him firmly at the wheel.

"Avery, answer my question. What do you want?"

"Touch me, Luc. With your tongue." Avery rolled her hips against his erection, mercilessly taunting his control.

Luc growled. "I will touch you, thank you for your permission, but I will decide how."

Avery might be shy, but it appeared she had a bit of siren in her. And he was just the man to make her sing.

Whoever designed her dress should be given a medal. He'd memorized the intricate details as she walked from table to table. Convenient scoops along the side of the bodice revealed a little side breast — provocative, but not enough to be scandalous. The exposed skin was like a magnet, pulling the back of his hand against her and feathering his touch down her gentle curves. Goose bumps erupted in his wake. The thin fabric of her gown couldn't hide her puckered nipples. He pinched one and then the other. Her moans shot fire through his cock.

The leg-exposing slit couldn't be left unappreciated. He slipped his hand inside and traced the lace along the top of thigh-high stockings encircling her legs. Heat engulfed his hand before he touched her mound, driving his lust even higher. He palmed the arc of her firm ass and pulled her flush against his chest, anchoring their bodies together, trapping his steeled erection against her pelvis.

"Do you feel that, Avery? That's what you do to me. I can't remember being this hard. It's all for you, beautiful girl."

"God, Luc. You're driving me crazy."

He needed more. He wanted to strip her bare and spend hours exploring every inch of her skin. What made her moan? What made her wet? What made her come? But this wasn't the place or the time. Luc wasn't an exhibitionist, not that he minded taking off his shirt, but he seriously doubted bashful Avery was ready for that kink. Plus, he wasn't ready to share his girl's bare breasts or pussy with a random person who could walk by their shadowed enclave. *His girl.* Where the hell did that come from? She wasn't his, yet the overwhelming need to protect her as much as devour her surged through him.

The hollow at the base of her neck was ripe with her scent — cardamom, peach, and a meadow of wildflowers carried on a breeze — the same aromas found in Viognier, one of his favorite wines. He dipped his tongue in for a better taste. Moving down her décolleté to the cleft between her breasts, her scent intensified, acting like an aphrodisiac. Each nip with his teeth at the pleasure points along the way, followed by a soothing lick, extracted the most carnal sounds from this woman. Her honest, eager responses frayed his legendary control.

The urge to claim her mouth was as tangible as her silky skin. Not since Sydney had Luc truly kissed another woman. He hadn't wanted to, until now. *Shit.* It took every ounce of his dwindling willpower to not ravage her mouth, to connect with her in such an intimate way. None of the subs he'd played with called to his primal need to dominate like Avery did.

Luc pulled back, his mouth hovering over Avery's lips and his chest heaving like it was starved for air.

"What's wrong, Luc?"

Control. He needed to get himself back under control. He wasn't some horny kid hoping to get lucky with the prettiest girl in class. He was Master Luc.

"Just deciding what I want to taste next."

"I was just wondering the same thing. My lips are aching to taste you."

This was more than just the Dom in him being lured by a sweet sub. This was a carnal need to ravage her, possess her, claim her. Guilt wracked his system, calling to arms heady arousal, provoking a battle for control of his mind and body. How could he betray his wife's memory like this, aching to top another woman? But he couldn't stop.

He gently bit down on her earlobe, licked the hollow behind her ear and traced a path down the column of her neck to the center of her chest and inhaled. Each inch of her skin held its own nuance of her flavor. So far, he'd only explored a small fraction of her beguiling landscape. And he didn't want to stop.

***

"Luc, you're driving me insane."

Avery's chest heaved just trying to drag in a sip of air. That's what this man did to her — he robbed her of her ability to breathe. And he'd only touched her while she was fully clothed. Well, touch being figurative because he used his tongue and teeth in addition to his hands. And it was so good.

"I can't get enough of you. I want to explore every delectable inch of you."

Luc's husky voice was enough to make her pant like a dog in heat but when he dropped it to that melty lower octave and whispered into her ear as he cupped her sex and ground the heel of his hand against her clit, it was enough to launch her into high earth orbit.

Embarrassment flared as she realized her thong was soaked. She hadn't been this wet, ever. Including after she came with the assistance of B.O.B. Her favorite vibrator had nothing on this man.

Luc coaxed responses from her body she didn't know were in there, locked away waiting for the right key to spring them from their secret hiding place. Was this what chemistry felt like? She'd read about it in romance novels, but the real deal was so much more than her overactive imagination could conjure.

Her legs trembled uncontrollably from the rush of endorphins coursing through her muscles from the carnal pleasure Luc was serving up. If it wasn't for the wall at her back and the solid man at her front she would be flat on her ass.

He slipped a finger under the elastic of her thong and with one swift tug, it was in shreds on the floor. She gasped. Their gazes locked. Arousal, thick and heavy, poured from him. It surrounded Avery, giving her strength and confidence that calmed her.

"Breathe with me, beautiful girl. Nice and slow and steady."

And she did.

"Gorgeous. Your panties were soaked. Do you know how hot you are when you get this wet? Feel me, Avery."

His steel-hard cock pulsed against her as he ground it into her pelvis, notching her own arousal to the next level. Everything beyond Avery and Luc faded away. Her senses became attuned to every nuance about Luc — his musky, spicy scent flared her nostrils. Each line on his face held a story she wanted to hear, every inch of her skin he touched or licked or nipped came alive with potent electricity. Her eyelids fluttered closed, too heavy to hold up.

"I want to feel your pussy clench around my fingers as you come for me. Would you like to come, Avery?"

"God yes, Luc. Please."

Fingers slid through her wetness on either side of her clit, stroking her closer to that edge but not enough to blast through it. She moaned, and her head fell forward onto his shoulder as her neck muscles abandoned their post. Luc chuckled. The moans in her head must have escaped her throat but at this point she didn't care. A colossal orgasm was building deep in her core, taking over her body and mind, so that she could only follow where Luc expertly led her. Nothing around them registered in her consciousness. Luc eclipsed Avery's senses, completely blocking out any inputs he wasn't orchestrating. It was over-whelming and outrageously delicious.

A blast of cool air blanketed her chest as the weight holding her up against the wall evaporated. She felt exposed, vulnerable without Luc pressing against her.

"I need to taste you. Grab the light fixture on the wall above your head. Don't let go. Eyes open and on me."

Avery complied with his command, though she couldn't recall willing her limbs to move. Her body did his bidding as if her muscles were connected to his brain. A puppet at his mercy. She should have been freaked out by her lack of control, that a man could penetrate the protective barricades she'd spent the last six years in therapy carefully crafting. But this was Luc, and she felt too damn good to care.

Avery was mesmerized by the unabashed desire glowing in Luc's eyes as he lowered himself to his knees, slid his hand along her calf to the back of her knee, lifted her leg over his shoulder and grabbed both cheeks of her ass.

"Tell me to stop if you don't want me to go any further. It's your choice, Avery. You have control here."

She had control? Luc's sincerity was as plain on his face as his perfectly sculpted nose. Could she trust that if she said to stop, he would honor her decision?

She was dizzy with need. There was no way in hell she was going to not feel his mouth between her legs.

"I'm not saying stop, Luc."

He took a deep inhale. "You smell delicious, Avery. Sweet and spice, like Gewürztraminer." He caught her gaze. "I'll never taste that wine the same way again. It will always remind me of this moment. Of you. Thank you for that gift, beautiful girl."

With one languid lick of his tongue, he tasted every inch of her from between her legs, over her plumped folds to her clit. Her supporting leg shook.

Luc chuckled. "I've got you. Relax into the sensations. You taste so fucking good. I wish I could see you better. I want to see how pink you are."

"I'm not going to last if you keep that up."

"Don't come until I give you permission, beautiful girl."

"What? I can't control it when you do that."

"You can, and you will."

His tongue circled her entrance then delved inside momentarily only to retreat so he could suck her labia, first one then the other, teasing each with the tip of his tongue. Her breathing shallowed as she tried to hang on, tried to obey. Though for the life of her she couldn't figure out why she didn't rebel against his commands.

"Come for me, Avery." He sucked hard on her clit and plunged two fingers deep inside her channel, swiveled his wrist, and hit her G-spot. Her brain was officially offline. She was reduced to a bundle of hypersensitive, fully engaged muscles about to detonate.

"Oh God! Luc!"

Her pussy pulsed around his fingers, and she threw her head back against the wall. He greedily lapped up her juices and placed tender kisses down the inside of her leg. The smile on his face when he looked up at her was breathtaking. She was the one who had the earth-shattering orgasm and he was smiling? How was that even a thing?

He stood, reached up and gently took her arms down from where she still clutched the sconce, gently massaging the muscles to help circulation flow back into them.

"You're so fucking gorgeous, Avery."

She shied away from his gaze, embarrassed that she completely let go all over his tongue and face. Unease played at the edges of her brain too. How could Luc have this kind of effortless power over her?

4

They were halfway to Avery's house before she cut through the silence. "Thanks again for driving me home, Luc. It really wasn't necessary."

God knew he didn't have a clue what to say. Just because Avery wasn't his sub didn't absolve him of his duty to discuss what happened between them. The uncertainty on her face was a clear tell he should have dealt with her post-orgasmic emotions on the spot. Luc had never abdicated his responsibility for after-care. He knew better. Hell, he'd been better.

The trouble was Avery wasn't the only person in pieces after that scene that wasn't a scene. How could he help her sort out how she felt about their encounter when he didn't have his own shit together? Successful corporate lawyer, multi-million-dollar deals negotiator, Master Luc, yet he couldn't find the words to articulate what just happened, let alone guide Avery through what she was feeling. He was still savoring her cream, not wanting her flavor to fade from his taste buds. He wanted to discover her edges, to walk the line with her on them and push through the ones she needed to conquer. Wasn't that the craziest kick in the head?

He grabbed one of her hands from where they both lay on her lap and squeezed, needing the physical connection. "Avery, we had this discussion. I wasn't going to let you take a cab home this late at night." He glanced at her but quickly refocused on driving.

A light rain darkened the asphalt making it challenging to see the dividing line. Oncoming vehicles' headlights punctuated the dark interior shedding enough light to see Avery worrying her bottom lip. The same plump lip that begged to be pillaged. No. Kissing was too intimate — the sharing of souls, the exchange of life's breath. Sydney was the last woman he would ever kiss. He made that vow at her bedside the day she left this earth. No one would cause him to renege on his pledge to his wife.

Avery squeezed his hand back and didn't let go.

"Well, I do appreciate it. What sane, red-blooded girl wouldn't want a hot guy to ravish her in a darkened hallway then take her home? I like your brand of chivalry."

Luc sensed she tried to sound playful in an attempt to bridge the growing chasm between them that was more than physical.

Luc knew he was withdrawing. Shit, he was doing it on purpose. He couldn't lead Avery on. She shouldn't get any grandiose ideas about what their interlude meant. The interior of Luc's sleek sports car felt as small as the stainless-steel tank he'd crawled into to clean out after transferring the finished wine to bottles yesterday.

He withdrew his hand from Avery's clasp so he could have both hands on the steering wheel. Her back stiffened as she twisted her face toward the side window. Away from him. He felt like a dick.

"Hot guy, huh. I'll take it." He hoped to keep the mood lighter than the heavy shit digging into his brain, settling in as if getting ready for a long winter sleep.

He wasn't such a complete asshole that he could treat her like the women he usually played with. She wasn't a one-and-done sub. All the more reason why he shouldn't have manhandled her back at the casino. What made him need to possess her? In a dark fucking hallway, no less. At least she had a hell of an orgasm based on the way she collapsed into his arms. The way she effortlessly obeyed him in that darkened hallway indicated she trusted him on some basic level. Why did that make him feel like a superhero? Her honest, unguarded responses to his commands fed his Dominant cravings like no other sub had. Not even his Sydney.

A maelstrom of images filled his vision — the barely-there straps of her dress fluttering down her arms to reveal generous breasts tipped with puckered, pink nipples begging for his mouth, her golden tresses wound around his fist as he guided her to her knees in front of him, her fine features distorted in excruciating bliss as she flew apart on his tongue. Luc pulled the bottom of his tux jacket toward his crotch, trying to hide the bulge flaring to life.

"That's me on the right, with the red door and black planters."

Avery opened her door before the car came to a full stop. He grabbed her knee to gently press her down into the seat. "Wait there."

Light from the overhead street lamp revealed her forehead pinching together and a questioning tilt of her head. "Please," he added. She heaved a sigh, sat back, and plopped her head against the head restraint as if she was summoning dwindling patience. Not that he could blame her.

Luc shut off the engine, got out of the car and strode to the passenger side to open Avery's door. He took off his tux jacket and held it open for her as she got out of the car.

"Ever the gentleman, Luc. Your mom would have been proud."

It was a short walk from the driveway to her front door, but the temperature had dropped a few degrees and the wind had picked up, heralding a typical late-spring Niagara rainstorm in the distance. He laid the jacket over her shoulders and pulled her into his side. This time she didn't soften and mold into his body. Rather, she felt stiff and held herself apart from him.

"Please, Avery." Luc felt like a douche for not taking the time to talk about what just happened. "Let me take care of you for a few moments. It would be my pleasure."

"OK."

She allowed Luc to wrap her shoulders in his tux jacket, but she didn't give over completely to him. He still felt stiffness in her muscles, but she nonetheless let him touch her and offer a little comfort. He blew out a grateful breath.

They walked together up the steps to her front door. She fit perfectly against his side. In her heels, her shoulder fit under his arm. A simple nudge of his head and his nose could be buried in her hair, drinking in her sultry scent. No. That would be just piling on the torture, and he was near his breaking point.

Luc held out his hand when she plucked her keys from her clutch. Avery looked up at him, her eyebrows pinched together in puzzlement. He looked at her keys and nodded to his hand. Her mouth formed an "oh" as she realized his intent, and handed him the set of keys with the appropriate one singled out. He slid the key into the lock, opened the door, and with a gallant sweep of his hand, motioned her to enter. Avery crossed the threshold of her home with her head held high and her shoulders back. Luc was proud he made her feel worthy of being treated like the queen she was. He hoped like hell the next man in her life had the balls to worship her properly.

Luc's chest tightened at the thought of another man touching

Avery, tasting her, adoring her. Hell, the sight of Gryff's hand on her back at the gala made his fists tighten. Jealousy was foreign to Luc, and he didn't know what to make of the reactions this woman incited in his body.

Avery tilted her face up to him, confusion assuaging the heat he'd seen earlier in her eyes.

"Thank you. For taking me home, for…everything. You sure know how to get a girl hot and bothered, don't you, Mr. Christianson?"

"Oh, Ms. Lewis, you have no idea."

His aching cock throbbed, begging to push inside her wet heat.

The fire in her eyes returned and scorched each spot of bare skin her eyes grazed. With the tips of her fingers she traced his pecs through his shirt, down his chest, over his taut stomach to the zipper on his tuxedo pants. He could only imagine how velvety soft her tongue would feel enveloping his rigid cock. But, that was where the image would stay, in his imagination. A groan escaped his throat.

Luc lifted her wandering hand to his lips and placed a soft kiss in her palm. "As much as it kills me to say this…another time, beautiful girl. You can hold me to that."

The words were out of his mouth before his brain could stop them. He had no business promising anything in the future.

"Mmmm, indeed I will hold you to that."

Channeling the ingenue he remembered from school, her lashes framed her gaze. But Luc suspected that if he could peel back a layer or two of the innocent vibe she had going on he may find himself a seductress waiting to be awoken.

"OK, you're officially killing me." Luc clutched his chest in mock pain. "At this moment, I find myself regretting I need to be up before dawn tomorrow and out of town for a few days meeting customers. I look forward to resuming this…conversation."

He swallowed back his ravenous appetite to taste her again and shoved his hands in his pockets. The temptation to pull the pins out of her hair, twist the blonde tresses in his fist and haul her down to her knees was excruciating.

"Time will fly. You'll be so busy you won't be able to think about anything besides your new job. If you have time when you get back, you know where to find me. And don't forget our interview next week."

"Indeed, I do know how to find you, Ms. Lewis. But, if you think you won't be in my head the entire time then I need to show you just how wrong you'd be."

He took Avery's face with both hands and laid a gentle kiss on her forehead, behind her ear, on the slope of her neck. He wanted to leave her with the impression he was a good guy, not some jerk who only wanted to get in her pants. Well, he was both those guys.

He needed distance. Time to put his head back on straight. He couldn't offer this incredible woman what she deserved. That part of him had died in a fiery crash five years ago, and he'd been sleepwalking through his life ever since. All he was good for was a pick-up scene with an experienced sub. Avery needed more.

This incredible woman stirred something unrecognizable deep in his chest. Would there ever be a time when he could live again? Would he ever be whole enough to be the man Avery needed? Would he ever be able to let another woman hold his heart?

Guilt engulfed his system, weighing him down, killing any thoughts of a future where happiness thrived. Would there ever be a time where every cell in his body no longer ached with their loss? He dropped his hands from her face and slid his tux jacket off her shoulders.

"Good night, Avery."

"Safe travels, Luc. See you next week."

The statement sounded more like a question and the look of rejection in her eyes left him feeling like an asshole. He knew he was giving off mixed signals, but his feelings were twisting in his chest like a tornado spitting out random shit without care for who it hit or the potential damage inflicted. He quickly opened the front door and stepped into the cool night.

As he settled into the driver's seat, Avery's scent enveloped him like a cozy blanket. The short time she wore his jacket was enough to embed the material with her essence. He brought the collar to his nose and took a deep inhale. Calm infused his bones. That could only mean trouble.

5

Morning light didn't reveal any understanding for the roller coaster of emotions Luc had unleashed upon her last night. One moment he'd been completely and utterly focused on her pleasure, seemingly unable to slake his desire for her, and the next he barely spoke when he drove her home, as if he regretted rocking her world down that darkened hallway.

She could still smell his cologne-scented musk, hear the dirty words roll off his tongue, feel his strong hands caress her skin. He played her body the way he used to play his guitar — aggressively, sensuously, effortlessly. He made her feel like a goddess and extracted sensations that were the stuff of sexy fantasies, never imagining they could be produced in her body. Her nipples ached for his touch. The steel rod in his pants was a dead giveaway she did something for him too. So why wouldn't he let her relieve some of that pressure?

Luc's deep, authoritative voice had Avery's inner sub clawing to escape the sealed tomb where it had been banished years ago. She hadn't questioned whether or not she would obey Luc's commands last night. It was both freeing and frightening. She

knew down to her bones Luc wouldn't hurt her. Yet, when he had
pinned her arms behind her back, her flight or fight response
kicked in thanks to ugly memories that wouldn't go the
hell away.

It didn't matter. Between raising her daughter on her own
and taking the city editor role at the local daily newspaper,
Avery's plate was full. They would meet next week for their
interview and that would be it. Besides, Avery wasn't ready to be
anyone's sub. Not even Luc's.

Avery shook her head as if that would be enough to get that
man out of her mind. She needed to focus on getting everyone
out the door on time.

"Thanks for babysitting last night, Mom. Say, did you borrow
Grandma Catharine's silver bracelet and forget to return it?"

"Of course not," Sheilagh Lewis responded, indignity lacing
her voice.

"I wanted to wear it last night, but I couldn't find it. I always
keep it in the velvet box in my top drawer, but it wasn't there."

"You probably just misplaced it. If you had put it away properly last time you wore it, it would be where you left it."

Frustration with her mom's flippant response threatened to
cause Avery's neck muscles to pull her shoulders up to her ears.
She refused to let her mother cause her to second guess herself.
The bracelet was in its proper place last week. It couldn't have
walked away on its own. Avery attempted to diffuse the tension
in her neck by tipping her head side to side for a lengthening
stretch. Her usual morning yoga practice had gone out the
window this morning, thanks to a sleepless night tossing and
turning, trying to make sense of Luc's confusing signals and how
he coaxed a colossal orgasm from her body, so this was the best
she was going to get.

"Mommy, Mommy, look what I found!" Cassie came running

into the kitchen where Avery and her mom were cleaning up from breakfast.

"What's that, monkey?" She caught a glimpse of the large manila envelope Cassie was waving in the air.

"Can Mommy take a look, please?"

She held out an unsteady hand to accept the envelope from her daughter, trying to keep her face as neutral as possible. She gingerly took the letter from Cassidy's hand, careful to only handle it by the corners, closed her eyes and took a deep breath before breaking the seal to peer inside.

Don't you know it's dangerous
to follow men down dark hallways?

"Where did this come from, Cassie?" Avery tried to control the tremor in her voice.

"By the front door, Mommy. It was on the floor."

"OK. Thank you. It's time to go up and brush your teeth and get dressed for school. Grandma will help you." Sheilagh Lewis ushered her granddaughter upstairs.

Avery peered inside the envelope again to identify the other item she felt bunched at the bottom. She gasped when she recognized the scrap of lace — the thong Luc ripped off her the night before.

The doorbell chime made her jump. She opened the door to find Gryff standing on her front step, a familiar stoic look on his face that made her stomach churn.

"Good morning. We need to talk." Gryff entered her foyer and closed the door behind him. "Has Cassie left for school yet?"

"No, she and my mom are upstairs. The bus will be here any minute. I was just about to call you."

"OK. Let's wait for Cassie to leave and then we can

swap news."

"Unca Gryff!" Cassie bounded down the stairs and into the big cop's waiting arms. He lifted her so they were eye-to-eye and gave her a big raspberry on her cheek, causing peals of giggles to fill the room.

Avery called on her yogic breathing to calm her jitters. She couldn't let Cassie see her hands shaking.

"OK, sweet pea, you need to get on your shoes. Here's your school bag and lunch. Grandma will take you to the bus stop. Give me a hug and a kiss and off you go like a big girl. Have a great day. I love you."

Cassie took her grandmother's hand with a smile.

"Have a good day at work, Mommy. I love you too! Bye, Unca Gryff."

Her baby girl's sweet voice and beaming smile gave Avery a moment of joy. She thanked God every day for her precious angel.

The door had barely closed behind the pair when Gryff spun her toward the kitchen and urged her forward.

"Let's go sit. I desperately need some coffee. Do you have a pot on the go?"

Avery nodded and headed to the coffee maker to pour fresh mugs for them both.

"Thank you." Gryff placed his hand on Avery's to keep the brew from spilling over the sides. "What has you so jittery?"

"Cassie found a letter."

"What kind of letter?"

Gryff's tone went from friendly-Uncle-Gryff to all-business-Detective-Calder in less than a heartbeat. God, she hated that voice. She closed her eyes and pinched the bridge of her nose as she tried to talk herself down from the edge of panic. Avery pointed to the envelope on the table.

"A threatening one. She found it on the floor by the front door."

Gryff wasted no time shoving his hands into latex gloves. He was incredibly steady and precise as he removed the letter from the oversized business envelope.

"Shit. Sit down and tell me what happened and where these came from. Did you handle the envelope or the fabric?"

"Seriously? I know the drill. Cassie's fingers were all over the outside, but as soon as I saw my name on the front, I was careful to touch only the corners and used a knife to open the flap. I didn't take anything out of the envelope."

Here we go again.

Thank God for Gryff. He had been such a good friend through the very worst time in her life, and now when she needed him again he didn't flinch. He was at her side like always. She wished she didn't need him in that way, that they could just be friends instead of cop and victim.

He took a moment to examine the letter. "Interesting use of newspaper stories and headlines. Somebody either knows what you do for a living or is in the newspaper business too."

He held the letter so Avery could see it. "Any idea what this sketch in the corner is about?"

She shrugged her shoulders. "I've never seen it before. It looks like a dead flower of some kind. What's the dripping liquid? It looks like…blood."

A cold shiver racked her body.

He plucked the remnants of her underwear from the pouch and held it up with a finger.

"Is this what I think it is?"

Avery flushed at the sight of her friend, the badass detective, fingering her torn black lace thong. She shrugged her shoulders. "Yes?" Crimson brightened her cheeks.

"Care to explain, or do I even want to know?"

"They're mine. From last night. Luc and I...um...he...in a hallway at the casino."

"We'll leave that topic of discussion for later." Now he sounded like her big brother. "When do you think the envelope was left for you?"

"It wasn't there last night when we left for the casino, clearly, because I was wearing those. Not sure if it was there when Luc brought me home or if it was dropped just before Cassie found it this morning."

"Was the door locked when you got home?"

"Definitely, Luc unlocked it with my key. When we got inside we were...distracted and didn't turn on the lights. If it was already there I didn't notice it. We got back here about thirty minutes after we...left the panties."

Gryff pulled out his phone to take pictures and make a few notes.

"Should I be worried, Gryff? It feels like Cal all over again. But he's behind bars. Right?"

She didn't like the look on her friend's face. Dread felt like a boulder in her stomach. He took her hands in his, unabashed anger, determination, and sympathy all playing out in his eyes. She pulled away, banded her arms around her waist, and started to rock.

"No! Do not say it. He's out, isn't he? Please God, no, not that."

Gryff nodded. "The call I took last night was from a buddy of mine on the Hamilton force. Cal was released two days ago. Last night he missed curfew at his halfway house."

Avery gasped, and her hands flew to cover her mouth, shaking her head. "But he hasn't finished his sentence yet. How could he have been released and I not have been told?"

The room started to spin, the rush of blood in her ears

drowned out whatever Gryff was trying to tell her. Bloody hell. This couldn't be happening. Not now, when she was starting to feel whole again. Someone was whispering in her ear and stroking her hair. It was soothing.

"Avery." A familiar voice. Gryff. "You with me, sweetheart?"

His broad shoulders loomed over her, his handsome face pinched with worry as his gaze bored into her. She managed to nod to her friend as he pulled his chair closer to hers and sat in front of her.

"Listen, I know this is a shock. I was told last week he was going to be released. The conditions include that he can't come within five hundred meters or have any contact with you or Cassie. Otherwise he's right back inside for the remainder of his sentence."

"Damn it, Gryff!" Avery slammed her hands on the table and jumped up from her chair to start doing laps back and forth in her small kitchen. "Our lives are just now becoming normal and bam, we're right back where we were, looking behind every door, triple checking the locks, afraid of my own shadow. I refuse to raise my daughter in a constant state of fear."

Capital A. It appeared every time she scrutinized herself in a mirror or saw herself in her mind's eye. Not the classic scarlet letter everyone knew. That one would be much easier to get over, not that she condoned adultery. This A was a different shade of red. Blood red. Her blood. Her unborn child's blood. Thank God it was never her daughter, Cassie's, blood. That would have left her completely broken. The A seemed to pulse and glow with a life of its own, calling out to her, mocking the woman she fought so hard to become. This A stood for abuse survivor. It was how Avery identified herself, sharing top billing with being Cassie's mom. It would always be who she was. And that pissed her off. She was thankful the physical scars had faded with time. But her shame was still visible when she looked in the mirror. She was proud of what she had been able to accomplish in the past six years as a single mom, yet the crimson A still hung around her neck, weighing her down. Her life felt like quicksand — the more she struggled to rise above the mire, the faster it sucked her back down into the blackness.

Liquid welled in her eyes, and her voice cracked as anger gave way to anxiety then to sheer terror as memories of that dark time of her life flooded her brain. She pressed her fingers in circles on her temples as if trying to erase the images.

Gryff intercepted her path and hauled her into his solid chest.

"Nothing's going to happen to you or Cassie. We already have extra patrols going past your house and Cassie's school. I want to come by later to have a look around your yard and check on your security system. This is all just precautionary, though. I doubt that dickwad is stupid enough to violate the terms of his parole so soon after getting out."

Avery snorted and pulled back, so she could look up at her friend. "Don't be so sure. My idiot ex-husband has done a lot of pretty stupid things. I wouldn't put anything past him. And this obviously is a message directed at me. Whoever sent it must have been following me. I had a weird feeling for a while last night, like eyes were following my every move. I dismissed it after I caught Luc staring at me. Maybe I was wrong?"

Her body shuddered, and she couldn't help but scan the room and the locks on the windows. A cold chill came over her, like last night. But there was no one in her home but her and Gryff. Did she dare trust her instincts?

"Let's focus on what we know and wait for the lab report on this note and fabric. In the meantime, go on about your day. Let us do our jobs. OK?"

"You make it sound easy. I wish my nerves would listen to

you. I just can't shake this feeling…I can't even describe it. But it's not good."

"Try to remember all you've accomplished and how happy that amazing little girl of yours is."

Avery smiled at the thought of Cassie running in the school-yard with her friends. Happy. Carefree. Her precious daughter had been her salvation through arduous therapy sessions combing through the detritus left in Cal's wake. She vowed Cassie would never become a victim like she had.

"I know you're right. I'll do my best. This new job has my brain occupied so I won't spend every waking moment paralyzed with fear. It's a good thing. Speaking of…I need to get to the office for an editorial meeting."

Avery put their mugs in the dishwasher, checked to make sure every appliance was turned off, and flipped every window lock on the main floor. Once she was satisfied she nodded to Gryff, picked up her purse and computer bag, and headed to the front door.

They left the house and headed to their cars. Her mom waved goodbye as she pulled out of the driveway after seeing Cassie safely to her bus. Avery felt safe tucked into Gryff's side. He gave her a friendly kiss on the top of her head and said goodbye, ushering her into her car and closing the driver's door. Too bad she couldn't spend her day wrapped in his protective embrace. Cal wouldn't actually hurt her or Cassie again. The note was just him playing mind games with her. Right?

Damn it all to hell and back! Years after he was put away Cal Winters still had power in her life. No point even entertaining the notion of seeing Luc again beyond their scheduled interview. Why would a successful, gorgeous, put-together man want a single mother who had a potential stalker and a crazy ex who just got out of jail? He wouldn't. Period.

Sadness overwhelmed her, sinking into her shoulders, defeating her before she gave herself a chance to explore the chemistry between them. The way her body effortlessly surrendered to his demands both scared her down to her toes and brought her a sense of peace she couldn't ever remember feeling.

But she refused to relinquish control of her body, of herself, to a man no matter how incredible that orgasm was. Avery pounded the heels of her hands on the steering wheel, pain reverberating up her arms, reminding her of her strength and resilience. "I'm not that fragile woman anymore. I don't need a man to validate who I am or make me feel safe. I won't allow my power to be taken by anyone ever again."

A shot of adrenalin did a girl good. Her morose mood succumbed to the energy boost. She closed her eyes and took in a few deep cleansing breaths to bring her heartbeat down to a dull roar. *Fuck you, Cal Winters. I'll never be anyone's doormat again.*

Avery put the car in reverse, checked the rearview mirror, and pulled onto the road. Her peripheral vision caught an unfamiliar car pulling away from the curb across the street. Odd in her neighborhood. That cold chill snaked up her spine again, this time its grip was unrelenting.

"Do not get blood in my car, imbecile!"

"Yes, Avtoritet. I'm sorry. I didn't notice the rose bushes in the backyard, Avtoritet."

"I do not understand what Father saw in you. Why he protect you in prison? Why he make you part of my crew when you got out?"

The Avtoritet didn't care about the tone of voice used when

dealing with underlings. They were necessary. They were the muscle. They could not be trusted. Father taught well.

When the time was right Father would resume his rightful place as Avtoritet, not that he ever relinquished the role. They needed to keep up appearances, so Father could be released without challenge by law enforcement. Which was why the honorific was passed temporarily for safekeeping. He would be generous with rewards because his business would have grown under the direction of his loyal offspring and his honor avenged. Avenged for the indignity Father endured when he was convicted of tax evasion. A man of his stature jailed for such a minor infraction made a mockery of everything their family had built. When the time was right, he would be avenged.

It was fortuitous that an unforeseen opening to punish Luc Christianson, the lawyer responsible for Father's prosecution, had presented itself. The Avtoritet always profited from opportunities, planned or otherwise. Being in the right place at the right time was not luck, Father taught, it was diligence. And, having a creative mind to see the benefit to the organization was a skill honed by its leader.

"Tell me."

"She definitely saw the envelope and what was inside."

"Good. What was her reaction?"

"The windows were closed so I couldn't hear anything, but she was definitely scared. The message was a good first step."

A sharp thrill coursed through the Avtoritet's bloodthirsty bones. "Good. You have proven to be of some use to me. Lucky for you."

The front door of the house opened to reveal the woman and a man leaving. The man scanned the surrounding area methodically and kept his body in front of the woman. Just like a cop. They drove away in separate cars.

"The bitch does not look scared now. Are you sure it was fear you saw?"

"Yes, Avtoritet. Fear was written all over her face. I am very familiar with that look." The underling snorted, not happy his report was being questioned by his boss.

"Do not get self-righteous with me! It is because of me that we are using the woman. You are just a convenient messenger."

The underling schooled his expression, duly chastised.

"Who is the cop?"

"Fucking asshole. Detective Gryffin Calder, Niagara Regional Police. He's the cop who convinced her to press charges that got me sent up. They were friends in high school or something. She's probably banging him too. Slut."

"I do not need your juvenile commentary. I do not care what you think. Your job is to do as I say and report to me. I will do the thinking."

"Yes, Avtoritet."

"They are not fucking. They do not behave like lovers. Their embrace looked more like brother and sister. If you were more observant you would know this."

"Yes, Avtoritet." Disdain laced the man's words.

A loud smack filled the car interior, catching the man off guard. His head reeled back from the force of the slap across the face, causing the side of his face to bounce off the driver's side window.

"How dare you disrespect me!" Teeth were bared and the Avtoritet's voice sounded feral, guttural. "Drive."

"Yes, Avtoritet."

The underling gingerly twisted in his seat to face the steering wheel, lit the ignition, and pulled onto the street. His eyes checked the back seat often, unsure if next time it would only be a hand that struck his head.

6

L uc had spent the day catching up on paperwork that had piled up from the few days he had been on the road. He glanced up from his computer to see Gryff strolling toward his office.

"What are you doing at this end of town?"

"Nice to see you too, buddy." Gryff chuckled. "You have dinner plans? We could grab a bite then head over to the House."

Bacchus House was an institution in Niagara, for those who knew about it. The House was a members-only club for folks who liked to get their kink on in the safety and privacy of those who shared the same interests. The refurbished barn, which served as the main building, was perched on a ridge at the back of the Hunter family's vineyard, surrounded by stands of virgin Carolinian forest. The irony wasn't lost on the members — virgin forest surrounding a club where sexual fantasies came to life. That little fact just added to the charm of the place. Rick Hunter, Luc's dad, Billy, and Gryff's late father, Thomas, were the House's founding members.

"I could use you in a training scene. You look like you need to unwind."

"That obvious?"

Gryff always seemed to know when Luc needed to blow off steam. Gryff had mentored Luc when he and Sydney began exploring Dominance and submission all those years ago. After Syd and their daughter, Ella, died Luc took the requisite courses, honed his skills and earned Master status at the House. The BDSM community was a salvation. D/s helped Luc focus on something powerful within himself other than the grief that had a vise encasing his heart.

Luc and Gryff met a few hours later at a quiet bistro not far from the House. They both knew the place well — the food was delicious and they featured local wines. They placed their orders, but alcohol wasn't included. The House had strict rules — only two drinks were allowed on nights you played. R.A.C.K — Risk-Aware Consensual Kink — couldn't take place under the influence of alcohol.

"It's been great to have you around for more than the occasional visit. I'm sure your dad appreciates it too."

"Yeah, I've still got a lot to learn, but it feels right to be back home in Niagara and at Sky Hill."

"Thanks again for taking Avery home the other night. Did I see that spark between you two reignite?"

"Why would you ask me that?" Luc's forehead creased as his eyebrows drew together.

"You know I'm not one to butt into anyone's business, but I know where you are, and I know what she's been through. She's got a big heart except it's still not whole. She needs someone who can be fully engaged in a relationship. Not just a fuck buddy."

Luc's mood quickly soured. He'd had his one shot in life at true love. Sydney was the love of his life. She'd been it for him.

Now he was alone. Syd's death had shut down his entire being. Casual sex was all he could offer. And subs knew the drill before they entered into negotiations for a scene with him. When Luc played, feelings were never part of the scene. He'd buried his feelings with his girls.

"Why do you care? Is there something you're not telling me?" Luc's tone had more of a bite than he intended. What was it about Avery that made him go all caveman?

"Whoa, it's not what you think." Gryff held up both hands in front of his body and leaned back in his chair. "Avery and I are friends. Good friends. Nothing more. I helped her through a tough time, so I know what makes her tick. And I also know you, buddy. I know you're not ready to give her what she needs and deserves. She is a wonderful woman. I care about you both and only want the best for both of you. So, calm that shit down."

Luc raked his hands through his hair, leaned back in his seat, and looked heavenward as if to ask for guidance.

"Sorry, man. I can't get her out of my mind. I don't remember the last time I felt something other than straight-up lust in the context of negotiated scenes. Maybe it's because we've known each other so long that there isn't that initial getting-to-know-you awkwardness. But, you're right. I'm in no shape to offer more than a scene. She's a sub, right?"

"She is. But she's not in the lifestyle anymore. Just be careful. You hurt her, and I may have to take sides."

A chuckle softened his words; however, they both knew he was serious. Luc's curiosity was definitely piqued. He wanted to know more about the woman who invaded his thoughts.

"Why doesn't she play anymore? Something to do with the situation you helped her through? Is that why you think she's so fragile?"

"I'm not comfortable sharing Avery's confidences. If and

when she's ready to tell you, she will. For the record, she's not fragile. She's one of the strongest, most resilient women I've ever known."

Luc sighed. Gryff would never betray a confidence. He shouldn't have asked. Still, he wanted to learn more about what had happened to Avery between high school and now.

The mention of her name kicked up his heartbeat and sparked fantasies with her luscious lips and succulent breasts in starring roles. He could still taste her honey on his tongue, which emboldened his cock to act on his own volition. She awakened hunger in places he didn't think were still alive. The question now was, what was he going to do about it?

7

It was a crisp, clear night in Niagara Wine Country. The moon and stars blanketed the sky like they were close enough to touch. Luc and Gryff pulled into the long driveway that led to Bacchus House, inserted a member's card into the security card slot, and waited for the ornate wrought iron gates to open. Luc glanced up as he walked to the front door from the parking lot. Was Avery also admiring the night sky? He took a deep breath, filling his lungs with fresh air.

"Hello, Master Gryff. Hello, Master Luc. Nice to have you both with us this evening."

Both men nodded toward the impeccably groomed, well-muscled sentry who held the door open for them. Luc and Gryff went over the plan for the training scene while they changed from their street clothes into their leathers in the Dom lounge.

Marlowe Hunter met Luc and Gryff in the viewing room.

"We have three new Doms tonight. Two have previous experience at other clubs, the third is new to the lifestyle. He's a natural Dom and I see great potential in him. We'll be in the viewing room as usual. You'll take the sub through some basic stuff, nothing too intense. She claims to be experienced, though new to the House. Her name is Lily."

Doms and subs new to the House were required to participate in an introductory training program overseen by Gryff. Marlowe, Rick Hunter's daughter, now ran the club and was a stickler for protocol, training, and respect.

Gryff took over the briefing. "She's considering taking out a membership with us and volunteered for this training session to get a feel for how we operate. She knows our Red, Yellow, and Green safeword protocols. Her hard limits are permanent marks, blood, and needle play. Intercourse is a soft limit. As you proceed, I will be explaining the techniques and psychology behind the various aspects of the scene. You know the drill. Your sub is being prepared right now. Any questions?"

Gryff slipped into his Dom persona as easily as a favorite pair of well-worn jeans. Master Gryff was part of the essence of who he was. As a detective, he was an expert in stripping away façades to get to the core of who a person was. Skills that made him a sought-after trainer in their community.

For Luc, Dominance was part of the armor donned when he walked into the club. A force shield to lock down emotions. Emotions that would flay wounds that still haunted him. As a result, when Master Luc played, the foundation of his scenes centered on quenching baser needs with a ferocity he didn't dare unleash on an inexperienced sub. When they both got off, he was done. Cool detachment had become his trademark.

"I'm ready when you are, Master Gryff," Luc said as he slapped his buddy's back.

Luc exited the viewing room and entered the scene room next door.

Master Luc quickly surveyed the well-equipped room, planning his scene. An oversized bed with a simple red satin fitted sheet took center stage, a leather-covered spanking bench was off to the side, a St. Andrew's Cross dominated the back of the room, and a long counter with a sink and towels surrounded by every sex toy you could imagine ran the length of the room.

A vision invaded his mind and stole his breath — Avery's sweet ass bared to him as she lay over the bench, ankles bound, his red marks of ownership displayed so perfectly across her ivory skin. Back in high school, the lovely but shy girl was the subject of many of his lust-filled masturbation sessions. Sure, he'd had sex since Syd's death. But it was just that, sex. Avery felt different. He wanted more than just a scene with her and wasn't that a betrayal of Sydney's trust, her memory? Guilt washed over him.

He closed his eyes, channeled his years of martial arts training to find his inner strength and harness it. He took in several cleansing breaths as he quieted his mind and focused on the scene about to begin and his responsibilities within it.

"Are you ready for your sub, Master Luc?" The door opened and another perfectly coiffed and chiseled man dressed in the requisite leather pants and red armband signifying his role as a DM, Dungeon Monitor, pulled Luc back to the task at hand.

"Yes, Master Trent. I am."

Luc turned his back on the door and walked over to the toys to run his hands over a riding crop, feeling the supple leather, checking for sharp stitches.

The rustle of lingerie and soft breathing tuned Luc's attention to the woman in the room. Trent's heavier footfalls and a barely perceptible snick of the door told Luc he was alone with her. Master Luc was present.

Luc's breath lodged in his throat when he gazed upon the beautiful blonde on her knees. She was blindfolded, hands bound behind her back, head gently bowed in a well-practiced posture, awaiting his instruction. Memories of Sydney flooded his brain.

The hair on the back of Luc's neck stood up. Based on the roar that exploded in his head, recognition diverted all the blood from his musculature to his ears. What the hell was she doing here? There was no way Lily would follow him to his club in Niagara. They had played in Toronto, and she didn't know anything about him. She didn't even know his last name. Personal details were rarely exchanged in pick-up play when both parties understood their scene would be a one-time-thing. Anonymity protected Dominants and submissives alike.

Channeling every morsel of training he could remember, he shook off the chill that engulfed his spine, took several calming breaths and focused his attention on the sub who had placed her trust in him. He chalked Lily's presence in this training room up to coincidence. He could do this. He was Master Luc.

Only, it didn't feel like a coincidence.

"We're ready when you are."

Gryff's command through the speaker was loud and clear. He had to make this work even though he had unequivocally no desire to scene with Lily again. Luc deepened his voice, hoping to conceal his identity.

"You look beautiful, sweet sub. You are mine for this scene. You may call me Sir. You have been made aware there are Doms-in-training observing us. Don't think about them. Focus only on me, the sound of my voice. Do you understand?"

Lily's mouth twitched. Her head tilted toward him, processing the sensory inputs available. "Yes, Sir!"

"What's your safeword?"

"Red."

"Red what, sub?" He couldn't allow any break in protocol.

Everything had to be perfect to allow Gryff to find the teachable moments for the trainees.

"Red, Sir."

"Good girl. If at any time you wish to stop, you must use your safeword. There is no shame in using your safeword. If you want to modify what I'm doing without stopping the scene, you must use Yellow. You're welcome to use Green if you're enjoying something in particular and would like to increase the intensity. You have the control. The final say. I've been informed that your hard limits are permanent marks, blood play, and needle play. Intercourse is a soft limit. Do you want to modify your limits or have any questions?"

"No, Sir!"

"Excellent. Stand."

He placed his hand under her elbow to guide her to her feet. Being blindfolded with hands bound behind the back could be tough on the equilibrium. He knew Gryff explained that a simple gesture like this added a brick to the foundation of trust built between the Dom and sub. It demonstrated to the sub she was safe in his care. Not that Luc wanted to build trust with Lily, but he needed to remember his job in this scene.

Slowly, Luc circled her, invaded her personal space, observed every little nuance of her body. The pulse point on the slope of her neck quickened as he scanned her from head to toe. Her lips plumped and nipples hardened in anticipation. Luc hoped like hell she didn't recognize him.

He grazed his fingers down her arms to the fur-lined cuffs securing her hands behind her back. With a sharp click he released one. Then the other. The clank of metal reverberated in the quiet room as the cuffs hit the floor. Lily startled. Good. He needed to keep her out of her head and in the moment. He took each hand in his and gently massaged her wrists and forearms to get the circulation flowing again.

"Take off your robe. Leave the shoes on."

Without hesitation, she undid the belt and let the robe glide down her shoulders and arms, catching it in her hands behind her waist in a practiced move. She folded the sheer fabric into a neat square and held it on outstretched hands. Luc accepted the offering and placed it on the edge of the counter near the door.

Lily stood in the center of the room unabashedly naked. He stepped behind her, inches separating them, and traced her waist with his fingers. He outlined the jutting bones of her hips and glided his hands up her torso to cup her full breasts. Augmented reality so wasn't his thing.

He stroked the soft flesh, careful to avoid her areolas, and brushed the backs of his hands against the sensuous side curves and back down over her hips. Her shoulders and neck relaxed as her nipples hardened into little pebbles. Without warning, he firmly pinched both nipples between his thumbs and index fingers. Lily gasped and arched into his hands. A soft purr emanated from the back of her throat as pain gave way to pleasure.

"You like a bit of pain don't you, sub?"

"Yes, Sir. More, please, Sir," she said as she ground her ass into his crotch.

Lily knew how to arouse a man, but she also knew that topping from the bottom was not acceptable behavior.

He broke contact.

A barely audible sound of displeasure escaped before she could stifle her reaction.

"I'm in control here, sub. I will determine what you will receive from me and when you will receive it. You need to be punished for that lapse."

"Yes, Sir!"

Her breathing became shallow and ragged. Luc could smell her arousal. He took her elbow and led her to the sawhorse-shaped spanking bench. With a firm push between her shoulder blades, she lowered herself into position — head down, ass up.

Kneeling near her head, Luc placed her right arm in line with the front right leg of the bench then fastened her wrist to it with a fleece-lined leather restraint. He moved to the other side and fastened her left wrist to the other front leg of the bench.

"Do you enjoy being punished, sub?" he whispered into her ear. "Should I use my hand or a crop?"

He quickly stood, took the crop in his hand, and expertly placed a red stripe on her left ass cheek. Luc knew what she wanted. Lily was a bit of a pain slut, so impact play wasn't punishment, especially if he amped up the intensity.

Luc landed another swat parallel to the first, then rained down three more, careful to not hit the same spot twice and with just enough force designed to frustrate, not arouse her. He smoothed his palm over the marks and blew a whisper of a breath over the sensitive flesh. Her skin came alive with goose bumps as she sucked in a shallow breath through her teeth. It wasn't enough stimulation for Lily, exactly what Luc was going for. She squirmed, trying to rub her clit against the leather bench, striving for the friction she needed to take her over the edge.

"Stay still, sub."

"Yes, Sir."

She wasn't in the zone yet.

Luc repeated the crop-caress cycle five more times.

"Thank you, Sir." She could barely get the words out as she strained toward an orgasm that was a hairsbreadth out of reach.

"Don't come until I give you permission, sub."

"Y-e-s, Master."

"I'm not your Master. You will call me Sir." Exasperation laced Luc's tone. Lily's attempts to top from the bottom would provide ample learning opportunities for the trainees, but it pissed him off. Master Luc was always in complete control of any scene. Why did he allow her to get to him?

The problem was his head was entirely elsewhere. With every touch, every breath, every sound Lily made, he imagined it was Avery bent over the spanking bench. Finally, his dick came to life with the image in his head of a different blonde, not the one in front of him. Lily certainly wasn't doing it for him. In fact, he wondered how she had done it for him in the past.

"Yes, Sir."

Luc returned the crop to the counter and chose his next toy, forcing himself to focus on Marlowe and Gryff's trainees behind the glass. He selected a vibrator and stepped to the end of the bench.

"Are you wet for me, sub?" He stroked down her back with the pad of his middle finger to the cleft of her ass and through her wetness.

He touched her mound with the dildo-shaped vibrator, traced small circles against her labia, purposefully avoiding her clit. She tried to push back to get him to put it inside her, but he continued to tease.

"Patience, sub. I will decide what you will be given, and you will take it to please me."

"Yeeesss, Sir!"

"Is this what you want?" He pumped the vibe in and out of her channel. Lily matched his rhythm as much as she could, given her restraints.

"Yes, Master. Fuck me! Fuck me now!"

Luc knew he was not going to fuck her any time soon, in fact, never again. He stopped and withdrew the vibe until just the tip remained inside her. Her penance for continuing to top from the bottom even after his warning. Orgasm denial was effective punishment for many subs, especially Lily.

After several minutes, he thrust the vibe to the hilt, stepped back, and clicked a small remote in his pocket. The hum of the vibe matched Lily's cries as she squirmed more frantically, doing anything to push herself over the edge. He knew he needed to fill the scene with teachable moments for Gryff, the reality was he couldn't wait for it to end. That was a first.

"I haven't given you permission to come, sub."

"Pleeeese, Sir. I need more," she panted out as a sheen of perspiration surfaced across her skin.

Luc slowly, deliberately, walked over to the counter to pick up a smaller crop. He used the folded leather tip to trace patterns on the soles of her feet, up the inside of her leg, across her pert ass then down the inside of the other leg as the vibe continued to pulse in her pussy. A full-body shiver enveloped her as she clung to the edge of orgasm.

Luc slapped her clit with the tip of the crop. "Come now."

Lily exploded. But it was Avery's cry of "Luc" that resounded in his head. His vision blurred. Lily's blonde hair became Avery's blonde hair. Lily's voice became Avery's voice.

Luc tore open the laces of his leathers, sheathed himself, pulled out the vibe and positioned himself at Lily's entrance. He anchored his fist in her long blonde hair to give himself leverage.

"I knew you wanted to fuck me again. Sir." Lily's repellent smile and nauseating voice snapped Luc's attention back to the woman in front of him.

"Goddamnit!"

Luc disposed of the unused condom and fastened his leathers as he clamored from the room. He motioned to Trent to provide her aftercare. He couldn't stand to look at her. Luc barely got two steps into the hallway before Gryff barreled out of the viewing room.

"What the fuck?" Gryff's long strides closed the gap between them.

"Not. Now."

Luc tried to keep stalking toward the locker room but Gryff grabbed Luc's shoulders, spun them both, and slammed his back against the wall.

"Who the hell was that guy in there? Your head was completely somewhere else. We never leave a sub restrained and alone. What about her aftercare? That's not how I run my training class. More importantly, that's not how a Master treats a sub."

Luc put both his hands on Gryff's shoulders and pushed his friend backward against the opposite wall. "Get the fuck off me!" Luc spat in his friend's face. "I gave you enough to work with. Let. Me. Go."

Gryff was having none of that. He stood between the locker room and Luc, hands on his hips, his cop scowl on his face, effectively blocking his best friend's escape route.

"Not good enough. We've known each other too long. That was not Master Luc in there. Talk. Now."

Gryff softened his face and stance. Luc's shoulders sagged, his head dropped forward, and he leaned back against the wall.

"I know her. The sub. Lily. She's a pain slut. We played in Toronto, but she knows the drill — once and done. She tried to push for more, but I put a stop to that shit. Or I thought I did." Luc blew out a heavy sigh and sought his friend's eyes, for what, he wasn't sure. "It gets worse. All I could think about in there was what it would be like to have Avery on that bench." Luc shook his head, disappointed in himself.

"Oh shit." Gryff brushed his hand down his face. "Like I said,

Avery isn't into the lifestyle anymore. She's had too much crap in her life. She won't be able to handle your dark side. Get her out of your head."

Marlowe stalked toward them, jaw set, eyes wide and unrelenting.

"Master Luc. My office. Ten minutes."

Luc changed into his street clothes and headed upstairs. He stood in the office doorway while Marlowe surveyed the main play room through the large one-way glass that dominated the far wall. She kept her back to him. He'd never been called into this office for a disciplinary matter by Rick or Marlowe. Tonight was full of firsts.

"Sit down."

Marlowe strode from the window to behind her desk but remained standing, the power position. Luc knew that game well and knew who was in control of this meeting. He sat.

"Care to tell me what the hell that was about?"

"Not really."

Marlowe gave him a half smile as if she knew that would be his response.

"Let's try this again, Master Luc. Explain your unprofessional behavior with Miss Baranova."

This time it wasn't a request. He sighed, resigned that he needed to come clean. Thankfully, Marlowe accepted his explanation with a warning to not repeat his performance under her roof or risk his Master status. Masters were known for their expert self-control, and Luc was among the best. Until tonight.

He couldn't get out of the House fast enough, which in itself was a strange feeling. Something about hearing Lily's last name got his brain firing. He couldn't put his finger on it but felt it was familiar. He attributed it to an intense evening of confusing emotions.

Maybe Gryff was right. Luc wasn't ready to be the man or Dom Avery apparently needed. Avery deserved to find a whole man who could love her, support her, and guide her through her submissive journey, should she want to go there again. Losing control with Lily confirmed his friend's fears — he could play with experienced subs who would give him the release he needed without tampering with his finely crafted tower of solitude. He would uphold his obligation for the interview with Avery, but nothing more. More would destroy his carefully constructed existence. More would betray his vows with his wife. More would risk ripping his heart out again.

8

Avery arrived at Sky Hill to find staff photographer and friend Rae Powell's car already in the parking lot. She grabbed her purse, jumped out of her car, and practically sprinted to the winery's front door. Butterflies danced in her stomach, and not a simple two-step. It felt more like a complicated lyrical number with hands and feet jutting out at odd angles, poking and prodding her organs. She opened the heavy door and walked into the foyer to find Rae talking with a tall, dark-haired, muscular man. Luc. Rae's friendly face popped to the side of his broad shoulder to smile at her, kind of like a lopsided adult jack-in-the-box.

"There she is," Rae said. Her infectious smile beamed Avery's way.

"Am I late?"

Luc turned to greet Avery, and in one graceful, fluid motion reached for her hand, pulled her flush against his body, kissed both her cheeks, and granted her a smile that curled her toes.

"You're right on time, Avery," Luc said. That famous Luc

Christianson warm smile made the character lines at the corners of his eyes crinkle in a sinfully, sexy way.

And then there was his voice. A voice that could melt the bark off a tree, or the panties off a cheerleader, back in the day. A full body flush crawled up from her feet to the tips of her ears, blazing a path of heat in its wake.

"Gen's in the conference room and my father's on the line. If you're both ready, we can head in."

"Lead the way." Avery managed to get the words out despite her lungs apparently forgetting how to work. She could barely control herself near him. Rae smirked as they walked out of the tasting room down a hallway of offices. It completely sucked having a friend who could read you like a book. The fact that Luc never broke contact with her as they walked to the conference room was more than enough for Rae's imagination to ignite with all cylinders firing.

Avery spent the next hour asking questions about transitioning from one generation to the next in a small family business while Rae took candid shots.

"Thank you so much for your time today. You certainly gave me a lot of material for my story. I really appreciate it."

"Our pleasure, Avery. Any time," Billy said then hung up the call.

"Now it's my turn," Rae said to Luc and Gen. "Can we go to the tasting room to get an action shot of the two of you at the tasting bar?"

Luc swept his hand toward the door as if to say, "After you." Avery smiled and proceeded toward the door. As she passed Luc, he moved to her side and placed his hand at the small of her back. It felt warm, comfortable, protective. She could easily get used to that feeling.

They followed Gen and Rae to the tasting bar. Avery didn't

want to lose the physical connection with Luc, but she knew Rae had a job to do. She hung back as Rae set up the shot and worked the camera angles a few different ways. It was going to be fun perusing those shots to pick her favorite to run with her story.

The sun was starting to set so the building lights came on. She hadn't realized the time. Rae excused herself to head off to another location, and Gen said something about packing and getting on the road.

"Do you need me for anything else, Luc?" a young man from the wine shop asked.

"I don't think so. Thanks for asking. Go ahead and shut down then head out. I'll do the final lock up," Luc said. He looked over to Avery and asked, "Do you have a few minutes? We're working on a new wine I would love to get your opinion on."

"Sounds like fun. Tonight is grandma-granddaughter night with dance class, dinner, and a sleepover so I'm all yours."

Luc's eyebrow peaked, and his eyes darkened as he looked down upon her.

"Be careful when you say things like that to me, little one. I may just have to take you up on it."

A delicious, heated sensation wended its way from Avery's core out to each of her fingers and toes, leaving them aching to touch Luc's taut skin that hinted at the well-honed muscles underneath.

She tried to appear in control of her body, to come across as confident and playful. "You certainly know how to arouse my interest, Mr. Christianson." Instead, her voice squeaked like a horny teenager.

Luc slid his arm around the back of her waist and pulled her flush against his hard body. She gasped. Just being close to him had electricity zapping through her muscles, twitching as if they couldn't help but telegraph all her insecurities. So much for coming across as an all-that-and-a-bag-of-chips confident woman. To make matters worse, or better, depending on your perspective, Luc's other hand stroked up the nape of her neck, fisted her hair and pulled her head back exposing her neck while angling her face to look up at him. The flare of desire in his eyes both shocked and aroused Avery. Her body softened into him, as if each cell was drawn to his so they could merge into a single, radiant entity. She was awed to be the focus of this strong, successful, sexy man. It made her self-doubt shrink into the nether.

Avery's need to feel Luc's lips on hers overwhelmed her. Her breath came in short bursts as her lungs anticipated him stealing her air. Her nipples hardened as blood filled them and pulsed in time with her heartbeat. But, instead of claiming her lips, he dropped sensuous kisses down her neck, nipped the skin above her collarbone, traced a path across her jaw, and laid a trail of more kisses up the other side, ending by flicking his tongue against the pulse point behind her ear.

"God, Luc, that feels so good."

Luc's shaft pulsed against her stomach.

"I've been wanting to do this since you walked into the winery. You taste and smell so delicious. There is nothing I want more, in this moment, than to spread you on the bar and taste every inch of your exquisite body."

Avery stiffened. "We can't. Not here."

"There's no one here, beautiful girl, only us. Are you wet for me?"

Luc ran his hand behind her knee, under her skirt, and over her mound on top of her panties.

"You're drenched, Avery. I haven't been able to get your sweet taste out of my mind since the night at the casino." He ground his rock-hard cock against her hip. "See what you do to me? Finally having you in my arms makes me feel like I can pound nails with my cock. Have you thought about me, Avery?"

Luc's dirty words ratcheted up her already undeniable desire until it became a living, breathing thing.

"Every night." Avery didn't care that her words sounded more like breathy, wanton moans.

Her whole body stiffened.

"What's wrong?" Concern blanketed Luc's face.

"I thought I saw someone over there. Watching us, then they moved away."

"Just your imagination, little one. Everyone's gone home. It's just us."

Avery wasn't so sure. Her senses went on full alert, determined to prove to Luc she knew what she thought she saw. She wasn't about to explain to Luc that she had a sixth sense about her surroundings because her asshole ex-husband used to blindfold her and terrorize her. Nope, she also wasn't going to tell Luc she possibly had a stalker that may or may not be her ex-husband who had recently been released from prison where he was serving time for what he did to her. Those little facts would douse any flames before they had a chance to figure out what this insane chemistry between them was all about. Of course, that was assuming she affected Luc the same way he affected her. Damn, those insecurities had just come back and bitch-slapped her right in the face.

Snick.

Avery practically jumped out of Luc's arms.

"OK, I wasn't imagining that."

"Nope, you weren't. I heard it too. I'm pretty sure it was just Gen or one of the staff heading out. Let me go look and I'll be right back."

Before Luc took more than two steps, the lights went out. The last of the day's light had faded, so the tasting room was plunged into near darkness. Avery stilled, paralyzed with fear. Her thoughts swirled to those times when she was robbed of her ability to see her surroundings, waiting for the next blow to wrack her body in agony. But, that was in the past. Luc was with her now. She wasn't in danger. Unfortunately, simple facts didn't register in her body's muscle memory to quell the tremors that overtook her limbs.

"Can I come with you?" Her voice was barely audible yet her fingers gripped his forearm so tightly she was certain they would leave bruises.

Luc's head swiveled. Surprise registered on his face, but he quickly bundled her into his comforting embrace. "You're shaking. Are you OK?"

"Um…I don't like the dark. It kinda freaks me out a bit."

"OK. Come with me." Luc took her hand in his, and she grabbed it as if her life depended on it. She couldn't help it.

"We have to go down to the cellar to check the main electrical panel. Stay close to me."

Avery fought to contain a nervous chuckle. As if she would be anywhere but glued to Luc's side.

9

A very's shaking hand felt child-like in his. The emergency lights had come on, though they were not all that reassuring. They just threw shadows under the stairs, between fermentation tanks and rows of barrels. Luc could see how that could frighten someone who was already teetering on the edge. Good thing he knew his way around the building with his eyes closed. He squeezed Avery's hand tighter in an attempt to reassure her as they wound their way through the harvest room to the stairs leading to the cellar.

"You still with me, little one?"

"Yep."

They made their way to the electrical room. Luc reached for the industrial flashlight hanging to the left of the door. He let go of her hand and opened the breaker panel to inspect all the fuses. Avery glued herself to his side like she couldn't stand to be out of contact with him. What had happened to her to have her so frightened over a simple power outage? Gryff's words about her being brave and resilient were incongruous to the woman clinging to him. The mystery of this woman intrigued him as much as her scent had his dick protesting to escape his jeans. Clearly, something was rooted deep in her psyche to cause this extreme reaction. The Dom in him couldn't help but want to protect her, help her. But, Master Luc couldn't be the Dom Avery needed to get to the core of her issues because trust was a two-way street. He couldn't expect her to lay herself bare for him if he didn't reciprocate. Opening the lid on his neatly sealed up emotions wasn't an option.

Sydney was the only other woman who captured his imagination enough to want to peel back her layers, find out what gave her joy, what scared her silly, what made up her dreams. Guilt assailed him. It grabbed him by the throat and threatened to bring him to his knees. Yet, he couldn't force Avery out of his brain — her taste when she came all over his tongue, the softness of her body when she melted against him, her beguiling scent as he nuzzled the side of her neck. Their few days apart only served to fuel his imagination as to how she would react when he got her alone.

But, he had more immediate concerns. He needed to focus on restoring the power to the building and attempt to extricate Avery from his side without adding to her mental anguish.

"Hmm, that's odd. The main switch was pushed into the off position. Someone must have done that by mistake. I'll talk with the staff tomorrow."

He flipped the switch back and the building hummed back to life. "Everything's OK now. All except my hand. You practically crushed it." His joke didn't have the desired effect. "Avery, you're whiter than a ghost. Are you sure you're OK?"

Luc placed both of his hands on her sagging shoulders, hoping a little of his strength would infuse into her. "Breathe with me, Avery. Everything is fine."

When her breathing slowed to a more normal rate she looked up at him as if emerging from a foggy dream.

"Yeah. I'm fine."

"That wasn't very convincing. Look, I know you have had some…issues…in your past. Gryff didn't betray your confidence. He just gave me a heads up to be gentle with you."

Luc attempted to rub his hands up and down her arms to soothe her, but she jumped out of his reach, flames of anger shooting from her eyes. She put her hands on her hips, squared her shoulders, and leveled a glare at Luc.

"Damn him! Gryff had no right to say anything to you. I'm not some china doll that has to be handled with kid gloves. Yeah, I have a past that sometimes creeps into my present. Who doesn't? Gahhh!"

She spun on her heels and stomped toward the door that led upstairs, shaking her head and muttering expletives like a sailor.

Luc lunged and grabbed her hand before she made it out of the electrical room. "Whoa there, little one."

She stopped but wouldn't face him.

"I wasn't trying to embarrass you. You're right, you don't get to be our age and not have some baggage to contend with. I know you're a beautiful, smart, confident woman. But, I just saw a frightened girl who went whiter than a sheet at a simple power outage. It's my natural reaction to try to comfort and protect those I care about."

The words were out of his mouth before he could stop them. And denying them was impossible. Her insightful questions during their discussion made her brain equally as attractive as her luscious curves. A piece of this woman lodged in his gut, refusing to let go of the stranglehold she had on his thoughts, his emotions, his fantasies.

Avery's anger deflated as she looked to him. Luc opened his arms and she eagerly walked into his embrace. Thankfully. She sighed into his chest and the tension melted away. Luc felt like a hero to be able to soothe her anger and offer some comfort. But, he wasn't about to drop his quest to uncover what triggered her fear.

"Come on. Let's go get something to eat. I think we've had enough excitement for one night." Luc tucked her into his side and they made their way back upstairs.

He left Avery at the door of the conference room where she'd left her purse and notes while he headed down the hall to his office to shut down his computer and clean his desk. Before he reached his office door a shriek echoed through the hall. He raced back to where he'd left her.

Barreling around the corner into the conference room, he dropped to the floor beside her. "Avery! What is it?"

She was sitting on the floor with her arms holding her bent legs to her body, rocking back and forth, shaking her head and whispering, "No, no, no."

"Are you OK? Are you hurt? Avery, talk to me."

Avery snapped her head up when he deepened his voice. All she could do was point.

He can't stop me

"What the hell?"

Avery wouldn't stop rocking, her eyes bugged out and stared off into nothing, tears streaming down her face.

"Why? Not again. Leave me alone. Can't go through this again. Protect Cassie."

Leaving the note on the floor where it fell, Luc scooped Avery up, sat in a chair, and settled her onto his lap, cradling her head against his chest. She sobbed uncontrollably. Soothing sounds rumbled from his chest as he stroked her hair.

"Talk to me, Avery. Let me help you. I'm here and I'm not going anywhere."

"Cal...it's Cal...I know it is."

She managed to get those few words out between the sobs and trying to catch her breath.

"Your ex-husband? I thought he was in jail?"

"Was. He was released last week."

"What? Are you and Cassie safe?"

"Gryff thinks so but, after this note and the other one..."

"What other one?" Luc's voice got deeper again. This time it was anger ripping through him at the notion of Avery and her daughter possibly being in danger.

Avery recounted to him about Cassie finding the first note. From what she described, this one had the same hallmarks — cut out newspaper letters forming the words, a personal message, and a strange illustration of a flower in the corner. He stroked circles on her back until her breathing synced with his and the tension in her muscles retreated.

Glancing down, something on the floor caught his attention. Avery stiffened again as she followed his line of sight. He used a pen from the conference table to reach down to flip over the paper without touching it or releasing Avery from his protective clasp.

"Sonofabitch."

Avery gasped when she saw the photo. It was them in the tasting room less than an hour ago with Luc's lips against her neck.

"How...could...he? Where?"

Avery was visibly shaking now. She couldn't get out full

sentences and tried to push away from his chest and slip off his lap.

"Where do you think you are going? Stay right where you are. I'll call Gryff." Luc pulled his phone from his pocket and dialed with one hand as his other arm tightened around her waist, pulling her back into him, not losing their connection.

Luc ended his call. "Gryff's not far away. Let's get out of this room. Leave everything where it is. We can wait for him in my office. He'll call when he gets to the front door, so I can let him in."

Avery nodded and looked up into his eyes. "Thank you."

He looked down at her, imbuing as much protective strength to her as possible. He curved his palm to the side of her face and thumbed away a falling tear. She pressed her delicate cheek into his strong hand. Her show of trust humbled him.

He placed a warm, soulful kiss on her forehead. "Nothing to thank me for, beautiful girl. I meant what I said. I care about you. I'm not going to let anything happen to you or your precious daughter. Plus, you have big bad Detective Calder looking out for you."

Luc's cell phone rang, causing Avery to jump.

"Shh. It's OK. Just Gryff at the front door." He got up, placed Avery on her feet, and headed to the door. She was instantly by his side, slipping her hand into his. He squeezed her hand and she squeezed his heart.

Avery clung to Luc's side as he opened the door. She couldn't help but anchor herself to him as her world spun out of control. But, the moment Gryff stepped into the foyer she left Luc's comforting arms and leapt into her friend's familiar embrace. Gryff had been her safe haven for too many years. She didn't have to explain any backstory, didn't have to justify her feelings, she could just be herself with him.

"Come on, sweetheart. Tell me what happened."

Gryff didn't patronize her. He tucked her into his side and pressed them toward the conference room. As they walked the short distance, Avery recounted how she and Luc found the latest message. How she found her purse sitting on a chair in the conference room, right where she'd left it, but something was sticking out. The message.

"Was anything missing?" Gryff asked.

"What do you mean?" Panic edged Avery's voice. "I don't think so, but to tell you the truth, I didn't check."

Luc's hand brushed up and down her back, reminding her he was also by her side. She did feel better when Luc was close. Strength and heat radiated off him and enveloped her. Her very own man-cocoon. But it was a double-edged sword. Luc and Gryff were wonderful, supportive friends who would no doubt defend her and Cassie, and for that she was grateful. But damn she wanted to, no, needed to stand on her own hind legs, to fend for herself, and to be the mother her daughter deserved. After all, look what happened the last time she let a man take care of her. Cal drew her in with all the right words and promises of ecstasy. Then, little by little, punishments became more frequent and more intense for nebulous infractions. She was no longer allowed to work. He dictated what she ate, what she wore, what she did. The insidious downward spiral eroded her sense of self-worth until she no longer trusted herself to make any decisions about her or her daughter's life.

Gryff's voice brought her back to her reality. Reality sucked ass.

"Well," Gryff started, "the note's not likely to be much help. The last one…" Gryff stopped short realizing what he said.

Avery gave him a nod to tell him he could continue.

"OK, the last one was clean. The newsprint used to cut out the letters was standard newsprint stock. Your paper uses it and so do the majority of dailies and weeklies in the region, not to mention a few in Toronto. The ink wasn't any help either."

"Have you found out more about Cal's movements?" Avery had to force her vocal chords to work. They throttled every word, choking off her airway just as surely as if they were Cal's miserable hands.

"He's been a model parolee, checking in when he should. Other than last week. He claimed to have car trouble, though we haven't been able to confirm that. Based on the approximate time the previous message was likely left for you to find, it could have been him. We can't rule out that it was someone else or that Cal has an accomplice. We'll add today's incident to the mix, map out the timelines, and overlay his check-in times. Don't worry Avery, we'll find whoever is doing this."

Avery was only half listening to Gryff. It was as if she were back in the middle of that destructive relationship. Frightened. Small. Humiliated. Not the strong, smart, capable woman who had risen from the wreckage that had been her marriage. Hell, she hadn't even seen or spoken with Cal, yet he still had power over her, derailing her growing confidence.

She sunk into one of the chairs surrounding the conference table, propped her elbows on the table, and buried her face in her hands. This couldn't be happening. Not now. Just when she and Luc seemed to be reconnecting. Who wanted to be with a single mom with this kind of baggage?

She hated that Luc now knew about her crazy ex-husband and what was apparently a stalker. She needed to get out of here before he kicked her out. Oh, he would let her down easy, he wasn't a total prick. Still, the humiliation was more than she could bear at the moment.

"I need to get home. Cassie leaves for camp tomorrow and I've got a lot of prep to do." Not waiting for either Gryff or Luc to approve or disapprove, she headed for the door. "Let me know if anything pops."

Before she could take more than a couple of steps, a wall of muscle blocked her path. Both men stood in front of her, glaring down at her, shaking their heads in unison.

"Oh, no, you're not. You are not going anywhere by yourself," Luc growled at her with Gryff nodding in agreement.

Avery propped her hands on her hips, again. She was getting pretty tired of defending herself to a slab of testosterone. "Listen boys, I'll be fine. I'm not going to let a couple of silly letters turn my life upside down. And…"

"And nothing. We don't know how serious this threat is. It could be nothing, but we're not going to take any chances with either you or Cassie. Someone has gone to a lot of trouble to create these messages, put them in places for you to find yet not be seen, and not leave a trace of evidence. That sounds like a determined bastard to me. We don't know what he's planning next."

Gryff's cop voice was a hairsbreadth away from demolishing Avery's last nerve. He must have seen her frustration because he took a deep breath and softened his approach.

"Look, I don't want to scare you more than you already are, but I also don't want to take any chances."

She was so worn down from worrying about what Cal might be up to, and being hypervigilant every waking moment of the day, and most nights. Cassie's safety was her primary concern. Avery knew she would survive if Cal got his hands on her again.

But, if he hurt Cassie in any way, she would never forgive herself.

Gryff was her dearest friend. He knew what she had been through, and he would understand what she was feeling now. She trusted him with her safety as well as Cassie's. He would see through her if she tried to pretend to be superwoman and blow them off, so why delay the inevitable. The sooner she accepted their help, the sooner she would be able to make sure Cassie was tucked away safe and sound in her bed at her grandmother's unaware of the potential threat her father posed. She took a step back and huffed out a sigh.

"So, what do you propose?"

The resignation in her voice relaxed Luc and Gryff's posture, a little. They all sat down. Luc pulled his chair in front of Avery's, his knees wide on either side of hers, and took both of her hands in his. His warmth flowed into her, traveled up her arms then into her heart. This man oozed strength and self-confidence. Not in a scary way like Cal. Rather, it was grounding, comforting. Gryff pulled his chair next to Luc's, and they both looked her squarely in the face, through her eyes, and into her soul. Her breath evened out, and her heartbeat slowed to a more normal rate.

"You and Cassie are going to stay with me for a while."

Luc barely got the words out of his mouth before she pushed her chair away from his so she could get the hell out of there. Her panic was instinctual. Loss of control over her own environment sent her reeling like she was back in Cal's clutches.

Avery noticed the subtle glare Gryff sent Luc that told him to back off and let him handle this. Avery appreciated Gryff stepping in to rein in Luc's well-meaning but overbearing demeanor. Luc sighed heavily and sat back in his chair, giving her some breathing room. Gryff nodded to her vacated chair. She tentatively sat back down.

"Luc has a good idea." It was Officer Calder speaking to her now. "Neither of us want you to be alone at your place right now. Whoever is trying to scare you obviously knows where you live and work."

"Fine. I know you're right. But, I don't want to scare Cassie or disrupt her life. She's doing so well. The last thing I want is for her to remember what she witnessed with her father and me."

"OK. I get it," Gryff said, his voice gentling. "How about this — Cassie's staying at your parents' place tonight after her dance class. Right?" Avery nodded. "Once she's asleep I'll go and spend the night on their sofa. In the morning I'll take her to school. I'll tell her you have an early meeting or something. Besides, I can't resist your mother's breakfast." His mouth curled up with a mischievous smile. Her apprehension about the plan eased. A bit.

Luc leaned forward, placed his hands gently on her knees — not enough to anchor her to the chair, just enough to reconnect.

"With Cassie safe at your parents' place thanks to Officer Calder standing guard, you can come stay at my place. Dad's in Florida and Gen just left on a road trip for a couple of days. It'll be quiet, and we have an excellent alarm system. You can have one of the guest rooms all to yourself. I'll be just down the hall in case you need me."

Gryff stared at his friend with that determined cop glower. "You still have your hand gun?"

"Yes, my permit's current and I was at the range last week. Dad's rifle locker's stocked and I've got the key," Luc responded matter-of-factly.

Avery was taken aback at Luc's seeming comfort with firearms. Why would winegrowers have a need for guns? Luc must have seen the question on her face, so he explained.

"We're farmers and any farmer worth his salt has the tools he needs to protect his farm from predators. Mostly, we fire blanks to scare the birds away from the ripening grapes. Every now and then a coyote becomes a nuisance, and we have to take care of the issue before it becomes dangerous."

It was a plausible explanation and though she would never admit it out loud, knowing Luc had a gun and knew how to use it certainly went a long way to reassuring her she would be safe with him. She and Cassie were in good hands.

Avery took a deep breath, rolled her shoulders, and forced them away from her ears. It did sound like a good plan, for tonight. Then what? She wouldn't be comfortable staying at Luc's place without Cassie for more than tonight. But, she was exhausted and didn't want to be alone, especially at her house. She hated that Cal made her afraid to be in the home she created for her and Cassie. It was small, but she was proud of herself for being able to buy it. It represented her new life and all the possibilities awaiting her. Cal could rot in hell for tainting it. As soon as Gryff checked out her property and made sure her security system would keep them safe, she was taking back her home. She just had to get through the next few hours under the same roof as Luc without collapsing into a blithering mess.

10

The Christianson family home was built on the edge of the main Sky Hill vineyard, nestled beneath the brow of the Niagara escarpment. Moonlight barely lifted night's shadowy cloak along Niagara's rural roads. Luc took extra care to scan the roadside for unfamiliar vehicles before he closed the garage doors, safely ensconcing their cars. Nothing caught his attention.

Luc had earned his first black belt in jujitsu many years ago. The mental discipline of martial arts was at the core of his Dom persona. He understood when and where to use his skills and knowledge. It was rare that he considered using his ability in an aggressive way. But Avery brought out his protective instincts. Hell, he felt like he would slay dragons for her.

Luc understood he needed to tread carefully, to not be overbearing. He saw how that behavior just pushed Avery into her shell of self-preservation. Avery trusted Gryff. Luc had yet to earn that privilege, though he was never one to back away from a challenge.

Luc led Avery into the adjoining kitchen, deactivated the alarm and flipped on the lights. He pulled Avery against his chest, placing a tender kiss on the top of her head. She resisted him for a moment then softened into his embrace, clasping her hands behind his back. He loved how perfectly she fit against him.

Four big paws, nails clawing the stone tiles, made a sliding entrance into the kitchen, interrupting the quiet. "Someone's happy I'm home," Luc said. "Come on over here, Merlot. There's someone I'd like you to meet. Avery, please meet Merlot. Merlot, please meet Avery. Despite his size and guard dog training, he really is a big ole lapdog, aren't you boy?" Luc bent down and not too gently scratched behind both the dog's ears.

Avery snorted and kneeled down to offer her opened palm in friendship. "Lapdog? I certainly wouldn't want to be an intruder in his home."

Luc was delighted Merlot could help divert Avery's thoughts if only for the briefest of minutes. Even more pleased that she actually smiled. He chuckled when, after a couple of perfunctory sniffs, Merlot sidled right up to Avery and licked her face like she was a long-lost sister.

"Awww, thanks for the kisses, Merlot. I think you're pretty special too."

"Looks like you have yourself a new best friend." Luc beamed at how easily his family's dog took to Avery. Luc's dad always trusted an animal's instincts about people. He could hear the elder Christianson's words. "Animals can see through all the bull-shit people throw out. If the dog accepts you, then you're all right in my book." Luc couldn't agree more.

Luc opened the back door to let Merlot out to do his busi-ness. He couldn't quell his craving to have Avery in his arms, so he didn't try to ignore his staggering need. "You're safe here tonight with me and Mr. Guard Dog Extraordinaire," he whis-pered and gently kissed the sensitive spot behind her ear, breathing in the smell of her shampoo. Not a heavy scent, just a lovely light, fresh citrus. Avery relaxed a little against him as he rubbed his hands gently up and down her back. But, she was still pretty wound up and she had every right to be. He decided to make it his personal mission to help her unwind and try to forget about that asshole of an ex-husband and a possible stalker.

"Come on, beautiful girl. Let me show you to your room and get you settled. How about a bubble bath while I make us some dinner?" He took her hand to lead her upstairs, but she wouldn't budge. "Are you OK?" He looked back but didn't see fear. The warmth and tenderness in her eyes swallowed him whole.

"Thank you, Luc."

"You don't have to thank me, little one. I wish it wasn't these circumstances that brought us here together. I know I'll sleep much better knowing you and Cassie are safe. I also know you're dealing with a lot right now. I can be a little…demanding. That's why I don't want to force anything between us. You can stay here as long as you like, no pressure. I hope you know that."

He was pleased to see her nod her head, even if it was a bit tentative. He also saw a flash of heat cross her gaze and her head tilt to the side as if she was debating whether or not to ask something.

"Don't mistake my offer of our guest room as lack of desire on my part. Nothing could be further from the truth. I've wanted you in my bed, under me, me inside you, since we bumped into each other at the Vintner's Awards. Long before that, too, if truth be told."

He watched her pupils dilate, the pulse point on her neck throbbed to a faster beat and her face flushed. Mmmm. She wanted him too.

"I know you're scared about the notes and what they could mean. I get that. I can be patient, beautiful girl. It's taking all my control not to haul you off to my bed right now, but you're worth the wait."

She hesitated for a moment before responding. "I appreciate your concern, but I'm not a china doll you and Gryff need to protect and coddle. Yes, I've been through more crap than I think anyone should have to go through, but I'm also a strong, independent woman because of that crap. I'm not going to break. I'll have my moments, don't get me wrong, but I'm proud of who I've become and who Cassie is becoming. Enough about all that. Now, what was that about a bubble bath?"

Relief washed over Luc as he led her to the master bathroom. Relief and admiration. This woman continued to amaze him with her resilience and determination. Fuck that was sexy.

"Gen brought back these foaming salts from a region in New Zealand that's famous for its thermal spas. Would you like to try some in your bath?" He opened the bottle and held it for her to smell. She closed her eyes, took a sniff, and a low moan of pleasure sounded from her throat and reverberated deep in his groin.

"Smells heavenly. She won't mind?"

"I think she'd be happy it helped you feel better. She said this particular mix is supposed to be calming, centering."

"Well, if that's the case, yes please."

There was a glimmer of joy in her eyes, yet it disappeared as quickly as it appeared. It made his heart ache to know this gorgeous creature had been hurt by someone she should have been able to trust. He didn't know the details, however, based on what he had witnessed at the winery, it must have been bad. In Luc's book, a few years in jail was hardly enough punishment for a man who hurt a woman. A woman, especially this woman, deserves to be respected, cherished, and well loved every single day so she flourishes to become her glorious self. He'd watched Sydney blossom and Ella was starting to shine before they were taken from him. He let out a heavy sigh. Would the ache in his soul ever not be suffocating? Tendrils of guilt strangled his heart, constricting the life out of any hope for anything more than a quick fuck with Avery. He couldn't be the man she needed. How could she trust him enough to open up to him but not expect the same in return? That would necessitate unlocking the carefully crafted box of feelings he would rather leave undisturbed in the pit of roiling turmoil at the base of his gut. Undisturbed and untethered to his current life alone.

"Luc? Are you OK?"

He stole a glance behind himself as he adjusted the water temperature to find Avery's gaze locked on him. She looked concerned for him. How crazy was that? With everything going on in her life she was worried about him. That was not how this was going to go.

"You don't need to worry about me, little one. I was just thinking how much I'm going to enjoy taking care of you tonight. Will you permit me that pleasure?" The words were out of his mouth before he could analyze them or determine their potential impact.

There was that flash of joy and unmistakable heat in her eyes. It lasted a little bit longer this time, and her shoulders eased a little bit more.

"I don't know what I did to deserve this wonderful VIP treatment, Luc Christianson. But, I'm sure as hell not going to look a gift horse in the mouth."

"Are you calling me a horse?" He smiled broadly, his tone full of sarcasm, trying to lighten his mood as much as hers. She blushed again. Damn she got to him when she blushed.

"Ha! Smart-ass. Go on." Avery made a sweeping motion toward the bathroom door with the back of her hands. "Get outta here so I can soak a while."

Luc headed downstairs to fix them something to eat and open a bottle of wine. Unquestionably, he didn't want to leave her alone in that oversized tub but understood she was probably wrung out from the events of today. She was headed for a major adrenaline crash. A little time by herself, safe, in his tub could melt the anxiety away. The time would also allow him to rein in his inner beast. There was no doubt Avery ignited his Dom side with a force he didn't want to acknowledge. Whatever had happened to her left residual wounds she wasn't ready to bury, and the Dom in him was compelled to take her to those barriers and help her break them down. To give her what she needed, not what she thought she wanted. *What did he need?*

His thoughts shifted to Sydney. Syd hadn't run when Luc let his Dominant side out of his closely guarded cage. Quite the opposite. She'd learned from it, thrived in it, loved it. Luc took Syd to subspace, often. That place where sensation was king and the ability to think or make a decision evaporated into the haze of carnal pleasure. It was a safe place born from an intimate bond based in mutual trust and respect where an experienced Dom could take a sub in his care. It was always such an incredible sensation for both of them. More often than not, Luc entered top-space, the Dom's equivalent, where he was so focused on his sub's every breath, movement, reaction, and, of course, her ultimate pleasure, all other sensory inputs outside the scene faded away. The moment existing for only the Dom and his sub. His heart grew heavy again. He missed his girls so much. He missed being enveloped in their love.

Avery was the first woman since Syd to call to Luc in such a primal way. His body thrummed with energy when she responded so beautifully, so effortlessly to his commands. He imagined on more than one occasion what Avery would look like when she flew into subspace — her cool blue eyes warmed with internal flames coursing through her body while her sensual lips formed words of passion. He imagined her begging him to allow her to come and his cock responded accordingly. He wanted to give the gift of ultimate pleasure to Avery. Avery was different. She rocked him to the core of his soul.

Luc let Merlot back into the house, locked up, and set the alarm. He took the stairs two at a time, eager to drink her in. He stood in the doorway of the bathroom, leaning a shoulder against the door frame, a glass of Sky Hill Sauvignon Blanc in each hand. He was mesmerized. Fluffy white bubbles covered her luscious body. Ear buds sat in her ears, her eyes were closed, and her head nodded as crimson-painted toes made waves in the bubbly water from tapping out the beat of some pretty rockin' music. He felt his grin widen as she mouthed the lyrics with the occasional air guitar for emphasis.

Blood found its way to his growing cock. Straight up lust he could handle. It was the warring emotions batting his heart back and forth like a tennis ball that had his gut in knots. Which team would win was anyone's guess at this point. Would it be the growing need to unravel this woman, or would it be bone-crushing guilt for even considering there could be another woman who had the power to infiltrate his soul?

11

B liss. Avery finally relaxed, thanks to Luc. A cool wet nose bumped her hand that was hanging over the edge of the tub. Her mouth curled up in a smile, and she gently rested her hand on the dog's head. Animals knew when their humans were out of sorts. Her cat, Mr. Chester, hadn't left her side while she quickly packed her overnight bag. Though she wasn't Merlot's human, the sweet dog apparently had adopted her for the evening. Slowly, reluctantly, she opened her eyes to find she wasn't the only human in the room.

Avery startled, sending water and bubbles over the side of the tub. She yanked the ear buds from her ears and quickly scanned up and down her body to make sure strategically placed bubbles covered her private parts.

"Luc! You scared the shit out of me."

Luc had the nerve to chuckle as an indignant, badass guard dog started to contort his body. "Incoming!" Luc warned. Merlot let it fly. He shook from nose to tail, expelling the water and bubbles that had sloshed over the side of the tub and onto his head. By the time Merlot was dry, Luc, the floor, and walls were drenched. Luc sat on the edge of the tub and gently wiped the bubble blob perched on Avery's slender nose. She burst out laughing, sending more water and bubbles over the side and all over Luc.

"Sorry, beautiful girl. I brought you a glass of wine, but you looked so into whatever you're listening to I didn't want to disturb you." He didn't try to be inconspicuous with his admiring gaze as it swept up and down the length of the tub. "Merlot, you make a terrible wingman."

The dog barked, wagged his tail, and took off downstairs.

"Oh, poor puppy. He didn't mean to cause such a commotion. Wine sounds perfect. Thank you." She very carefully reached for the glass so the bubble mask remained intact.

To those in the wine business, the liquid in the glass was more than just beverage alcohol. Without thinking, Avery performed the ritual of reverently discovering the nuances of the wine. She swirled it in the bowl of the glass to release the aromatics, closed her eyes, brought the rim of the glass to her nose and took a deep inhale. Then she put the glass to her lips, took a small sip, and rolled it around in her mouth, coating all her taste buds. *Mmm. Lovely notes of fresh cut grass, lemon, and lime. Balanced yet substantial mouth-feel. A great sipper but would also be delish with food.* Avery couldn't help herself. Wine had become more intellectual for her since she started on the wine beat — every glass evaluated on its merits rather than simply enjoying. She couldn't decide if that was a good thing or not.

Luc must have decided his new favorite pastime was watching Avery taste wine. Her lips throbbed under his intense gaze as it locked onto her lips. Her clit pulsed in time with her galloping heartbeat as she valiantly tried to bring her breathing back under some semblance of control.

"Mmm. Your Sauv Blanc is delicious. Fresh, crisp, lemon and

lime, with the right balance of herbal notes. Bet it's a terrific match with seafood."

When he didn't respond her eyes popped open. "Luc, you still here?"

"Yes, Avery." The deep timber of his voice made her nipples harden like granite. His teasing fingers created fanciful swirls with the bubbles covering her body, a peek of upper thigh here, a hint of cleavage there. He hadn't even touched her yet and every molecule of her body was straining to feel his skin against hers.

"You're making me uncomfortable. You with all your clothes on, staring at me like that, and me all naked and covered in bubbles." Her mouth curled up on one side as her gaze wandered up the length of his body and settled on his eyes.

"You're so beautiful. There's nothing I would love more than to join you. I do have to get out of these wet clothes anyway."

"Well, we wouldn't want you to catch a chill by staying in wet clothes. You'd best be getting out of them." She took another sip of wine and sat back to enjoy what was most certainly going to be a hell of a show.

Luc placed his glass on the edge of the tub and started to unbutton his shirt. Slowly. Each piece of skin he exposed notched up her heart rate another level. By the time the shirt was unbuttoned and he was pulling the tails from his pants she thought for sure he'd be able to see her heart thumping in her chest. He peeled the shirt off his shoulders. It slid down his arms and he held it out in one hand. With all the dramatic flare of the Men from Downunder he opened his hand to let the shirt float to the floor.

"Very smooth, Mr. Christianson."

"I'm glad you are suitably impressed, Ms. Lewis. I've practiced that move a few times."

"I'm sure you have. But, can I just say, wow."

Her eyes were riveted to his hands as they worked the button and zipper on his trousers. Until the unmistakable bulge outlined by his body-hugging boxer briefs left nothing for her imagination. Holy hell. The purplish head poked out from the top of the waistband, glistening with a drop of pre-come that made her mouth water. She'd never seen a cock that big. Not that she'd seen that many, but still. Her core ached at the thought of him stretching her open, pushing his way inside, claiming her.

"Looks like there's room for two in this tub. Wouldn't want you to get lonely in there." Luc pushed the boxer briefs down his legs and kicked them aside.

"I guess we should take full advantage," Avery said. Apprehension morphed into anticipation. She couldn't help but lick her lips, hopeful she wasn't drooling. God, but the man was beautiful and didn't seem at all bashful about showing off his body. He clearly took care of himself, could even put a lot of younger guys to shame. Pretty damn hot for a guy in his late thirties. She languidly gazed up at him, unable and unwilling to avert her eyes as he climbed into the tub.

"Now I'm the one blushing," Luc said. He eased himself into the water at the opposite end and tenderly lifted her legs and laid them down on top of his. "I'm glad you like what you see. I told you there was room for two." He rested his upper shoulders against the end of the tub, reached for his glass, took a sip, and let out a relaxing sigh.

Warmth from his big body drifted into hers. She took another sip of wine, closed her eyes, and laid her head back on the edge of the tub. A gentle caress slid over her foot. He placed her heel on his chest and settled into a firm, sensuous rhythm, gliding both hands up her calf then back down to work his thumbs into the arch, ending the stroke with a little tug on each toe. She sighed and slid a little deeper into the water as any remnants of stress from the day evaporated.

"You look so relaxed. I'd like to see what other looks I can put on that gorgeous face of yours, little one." He brought that foot closer to his mouth and cascaded kisses over the inside of her ankle, up her calf, and back down the outside.

"That feels heavenly."

"I'm glad to see you're easy to please."

Avery raised an eyebrow and gave Luc a playfully taunting look. "Don't be so sure of yourself, mister. I'm not that easy."

"Ha! Far be it from me to ever suggest Ms. Lewis was easy."

He finished with the first foot, gently laid it down on his rock-hard erection. Avery couldn't mistake his playfulness for lack of desire. He picked up her other foot and continued his sensual therapy.

"So, tell me, what were you listening to when I so rudely interrupted you?"

"If this is an interruption, you're welcome anytime." She laid her head back against the tub again to savor his ministrations before she answered. "Probably not what you would expect."

"How so?"

"Avenged Sevenfold, Soundgarden, Foo Fighters, Seether. Stuff like that."

"You're kidding, right?"

She opened her eyes and sat up, pulling her foot from his grasp. "Not kidding at all. I've been a rocker chick since high school. A certain local band introduced me to the wonders of Led Zeppelin, AC/DC, Pink Floyd, Black Sabbath, to name a few. I've been hooked ever since."

"Wow. I never would have pegged you for a hard rock fan."

"Well," Avery tapped her index finger against her lips, "there was this cute guy in high school who helped me to hear the nuances and musicality of hard rock. It's more complex than it appears on the surface. I helped him with English lit, he helped me with music appreciation."

"That sounds oddly familiar."

"Whenever I need to muster my inner warrior goddess I crank the volume and let the music take over my body. I know I'm not invincible but the guitar riffs, intense bass line, powerful drums, and passionate lyrics grab me by the throat and infuse me with an inner strength I can't describe. It's soulful for me."

Water sloshed as Luc scooped under her butt and in a deft show of strength pulled her toward him so she was straddling his lap, her pussy lined up perfectly with his shaft. It pulsed against her labia as he ground his pelvis up into hers, pressing against her clit with torturous precision. Luc's chocolate eyes grew darker as lust crowded out all other emotions.

"I need to taste you again, Avery. Once was not enough."

Luc slid a hand up her back to cradle the back of her head, threading her hair between his fingers. Then he tugged, angling her head, leaving her neck exposed for the taking. Avery tensed and gasped against the pinpricks of pain in her scalp.

"Wait for it, beautiful girl."

Then she felt it. Shards of pain ignited every nerve fiber in her scalp followed by fissions of exquisite pleasure cascading down through her body, somehow morphing into a powerful need that left her pussy aching to be filled. The expression on her face must have given her away because the smirk he gave her was smug. He knew exactly what he was doing. Not that she was complaining. She hadn't ever been this aroused during sex, and he hadn't even gotten to the good stuff yet.

"There it is. You feel it now don't you, Avery? I'll bet your pussy is wet and plump and begging to be filled with my cock."

What the hell? Pain didn't equate to pleasure. Pain was pain. Period. What was Luc doing to her?

Luc trailed his tongue along the shell of her ear, eliciting shivers like a ticklish school girl. He sucked the lobe between his lips then bit. Avery moaned. The sting of Luc's bite zipped a trail of fire directly to her clit.

"You like that, don't you? Don't try to figure it out. Just feel it. Let it take you where your body wants to go."

More water and bubbles overflowed the tub onto the bathroom floor, but Avery was oblivious. All she could do was soak in his energy as it flowed into her while he played her body like a maestro taking her higher and higher to the inevitable crescendo.

"Oh, Luc. I've never…My God…It feels…" Coherent thought eluded her.

"That's it, beautiful girl. Come for me." Luc reached between them and pressed his thumb on her clit. "Come for me and know who made you feel like the goddess you are."

She floated away to another plane that she had only read about, incredulous at the sensations. Layers of color swaddled her in a calm acceptance of herself as a sexual being. How could she have had sex and never experienced this euphoria? A girl could crave this feeling.

Luc did this to her. For her.

How could she ever go back to basic sex? Wait. They hadn't even had full on sex yet. Could it get even better than this? She wouldn't survive.

She opened her eyes to find her face nestled against a slab of muscle. And it smelled so good. If only she had muscle control she'd stick out her tongue and taste that expanse of male skin. Bet he would taste better than her favorite Cabernet Franc — smooth, complex with a dash of spice to keep things interesting. Yum!

Heat radiated from his body, keeping her warm. Every point of contact simmered like embers of a campfire. A bit of stoking and they would ignite into an inferno. Again. Still? The head of his enormous cock bumped into her belly. He was still hard. All his attention had been lavished on her, bringing her ultimate pleasure. But it was more than an otherworldly orgasm — she felt worshiped, sexy, and completely at Luc's mercy. Avery's breath caught in her throat as Luc lifted them both out of the tub and carried her to the bedroom, snagging a cozy, fluffy towel along the way.

Luc had been giving off alpha male vibes his entire life, but they hadn't been focused on her, until recently. Her body ignited whenever he was near. And her brain shut down. She'd been down that road before and it ended horribly. She had the scars to prove it. Problem was, she had tried dating vanilla guys, but they didn't make it past first base. They simply didn't fire her engines. Luc was a Dom, Avery was convinced of that based on everything she'd read about D/s. And man, were her engines revving on all cylinders. For him.

God, Luc awakened parts of her body she didn't know were dead. His voice, his strength, his commanding presence all wrapped up in a sexy-as-sin package made for a potent aphrodisiac. Undeniable. And that was a problem. Luc overwhelmed her and then she caved to his commands.

So many questions swirled in Avery's mind, keeping her from giving over to Luc completely. She knew about the monumental mind fuck that came with a D/s relationship. Was she ready to expose herself to that kind of intimate power exchange? Could she trust herself enough to believe she wouldn't get pulled down into the rabbit hole of abuse again? Was Luc the man who could shepherd her on that journey? Wait. Who said he was even interested in taking her on as his sub?

Luc wasn't Cal, he wouldn't physically hurt her. Her heart was an entirely different matter based on how he shut her out on the way home from the Vintner's Awards. That hurt. Was she strong enough to survive heartbreak should Luc get bored with her? The only way she would find out was obvious, and so cliché. But it was her decision. Every lame-ass overused phrase popped into her head — do or do not, there is no try, in for a penny, in for a pound, take the leap — yadda yadda. It was time, and if there was anyone with whom she wanted to break free of her past, it was with this man, Master Luc.

12

L uc's gentle hand on her cheek brought her brain back online.

"Hey, beautiful girl, where did you go? Put all your worries out of your head. Focus on me. Allow the sensations to surround you, envelop you."

Luc gently laid her down on her back with her legs hanging over the side of the bed. The coolness of the sheets sent goose bumps all over her skin. It was a sharp contrast to the warmth of the bath and the heat from Luc's body.

Luc leaned over her and braced his weight on his elbows. His rippling biceps had her rapt attention until he nibbled, licked, and kissed a trail down her neck and over her collarbone to the sensitive hollow at the base of her throat. Avery didn't even know about that spot, but the charge of electricity skittering over her skin clearly meant Luc knew what he was doing.

"You smell and taste incredible, beautiful girl. Even better than I remembered." Luc's words, and the wicked tongue that spoke them, banished all thoughts of her ex-husband. She was breathless.

Luc said and did everything Avery needed. She knew Luc to be a man of integrity. Gryff trusted him. That went a long way in her book.

Luc stood back. His eyes caressed her from head to toe. The intensity of his stare ignited a surge of fire that banished the goose bumps and left a trail of heat wicking across her skin. Avery sucked in a quick breath between her teeth. She throbbed with desire, surprised at herself for not feeling the least bit inhibited. She simply let his sensuous gaze lavish her body, sensitizing her skin in its wake. Intoxicating.

"Tonight there's no one to interrupt us. It's just you, beautiful girl, and me. I wonder how many times I can get you to scream my name."

"Luc," she rasped, "you make me feel like a goddess. No one has ever talked to me or touched me or looked at me with such… reverence." She blinked to fight back the tears welling in her eyes. This was too special a moment to be ruined by her self-doubt.

"Let me show you how much I want you to feel like the goddess I see in front of me. You're a sexy, beautiful, smart woman who deserves to be worshiped every day."

Luc leaned over her until their eyes were inches apart. He nipped her chin with his teeth then soothed the spot with feather-light kisses. He pulled up and captured her gaze again. She saw barely leashed, raw need but it didn't scare her. A calmness came over her that she hadn't experienced in…well, she couldn't remember when. She trusted him.

"Why did you stop…?"

He flashed her a devilish grin before his sensual mouth assaulted the hollow at the junction of her neck and collar bone. Getting his fill, he continued to the valley between her breasts, followed the curve underneath the fullness of one, up the side and back to the middle to cross over to the other breast, drawing a figure eight across her chest with the tip of his tongue, searing his path into her memory.

"Oh my God, Luc. That's so good." She had no idea that the side and underneath her breast was so sensitive. She arched to meet his mouth, no longer in control over her body's responses. She just felt. And she was OK with that.

Lips latched onto one of her nipples. Luc sucked and laved each one, sending waves of pleasure all the way to her toes. But it wasn't enough to send her over the precipice. His skilled fingers joined the fun, pinching and rolling each nipple until it was diamond hard. A flick of the nubs with his fingernail kickstarted an entirely different engine — pain was the fuel that burned white hot in her core.

"You are so fucking gorgeous," Luc growled. He shifted to bestow the same treatment to her other nipple. The roughness of his tongue against the stiff nipple was exquisite torture.

Just when she thought she couldn't be more on fire, his muscular thigh pushed between her legs and the heel of his hand pressed against her mound. She was so close. Then he pulled away.

"Luc, please," she barely whispered, unable to catch her breath. Every nerve ending was electrified and not under her control. She had never been awash with sensation like this. Ever. But, she knew this man, her high school crush all grown up, would be able to make her boneless unlike any other man could.

"I can feel your heat on my leg. I'll bet you're so wet for me, beautiful girl. But don't come yet. I'm not even close to done with you."

Alternating between playful and ravishing, Luc's mouth continued down her body, over her stomach to the sensitive skin just above her trimmed curls. Her breath quickened when his fingers found her wet folds. He knew exactly what he was doing and how high he was pushing her. He took her to the pinnacle of desire faster than she imagined was even possible. She needed to come. Now.

A primal rumble came from Luc's chest. God that was hot. "You're soaking. You're so incredibly sexy the way you purr my name and those little sounds you make have me so hard. I can feel how close you are. Your pussy is milking my fingers. But I haven't given you permission to come. Yet."

Avery grabbed his silky hair to direct his head. To hell with not coming. She couldn't take any more. This orgasm was going to be extreme. Now. She needed to come now.

He shook his head out of her hands. "I don't think so, little one. I'm in control here. I will decide what you will or won't take from me. Reach your hands behind your head and hold onto the edges of the pillow. Don't let go. Understand?"

"I can't take any more. I need to come. Now."

"You can and you will. Hands." Luc's voice dropped an octave.

She wanted to comply, wanted to please him.

"Yes, Sir." The words rolled off her tongue.

Avery gazed down at his gorgeous face. His smile accentuated his rugged cheekbones and the fine lines at the corner of his eyes. The wicked gleam told her he knew exactly what he was doing to her. A lick from her folds to her clit had her practically levitating off the bed. His chuckle reverberated throughout the room. The tip of his tongue traced circles around her clit, but never touching, not giving her the stimulation she needed. A finger inside her clenching channel had her screaming his name, begging for release. Avery used every muscle in her body to stave off a cataclysm. He had to let her come before she exploded. Death by orgasm. She could see the headlines now.

Luc settled on his knees on the floor and his broad shoulders pressed her legs farther apart. "Look at how plump and pink you are for me. Gorgeous. I couldn't see you the last time I tasted you and now I won't have you any other way. I want to watch you flush with arousal. I want to watch you come undone for me."

One finger became two, and he started to plunge in and out while his talented mouth destroyed what was left of her sanity. Luc sucked her folds, pressed each to the roof of his mouth, brought her to the brink then eased back. Again.

"Luc! Stop torturing me! Please. I need to come."

This man. Wow, this man knew how to extract extreme pleasure from her. He was going to ruin her for anyone else. Hell, how could there be anyone else after this?

"That's it, beautiful girl. Almost there." He continued his expert ministrations, playing her body like one of his guitars.

"Now, Avery, come for me."

With a gentle scrape of his teeth over her sensitized nub, she exploded. A kaleidoscope of color burned from the inside out, consumed every rational thought and external sensation in its path. She couldn't see or hear anything other than what was happening inside her own body and even that she couldn't put to words.

Several aftershocks later, she was able to unravel the jumble of thoughts in her brain. Mostly. Luc kept lapping at her juices, murmuring like a satisfied gourmand, drawing out her bliss. His head tilted up and caught her gaze, his eyes feral with lust.

He flashed her a mouth-watering, ear-to-ear smile. "Spectacular. I wish you could have seen how gorgeous you were when you came. Thank you for trusting me enough to let go."

"Isn't that my line, mister?" Her voice was a little hoarse from her screams of pleasure. "I'm not sure where I went just then but man, it sure was a hell of a trip. You, Mr. Christianson, are a very talented man with a thoroughly wicked tongue. Wow."

"I'm honored milady approves. Now, I can't wait to get inside of that delectable pussy of yours. Damn, I haven't felt this hot for anyone in a very long time. You're going to be the death of me."

Avery sensed his control had started to slip. He became rougher, more demanding. But this was Luc, she trusted him. He would never hurt her. He only wanted her pleasure, and his. So why did she feel short of breath? Yes, lust had her panting, but there was something else her body was reacting to.

She closed her eyes and tried to center herself. The nightstand drawer opened and a rip of foil punctuated the sound of her panting breaths. Avery wanted Luc inside her. More than anything she wanted to give him pleasure in return for the pleasure he gave her. She could feel his muscular legs pushing hers apart and his iron-hard erection pulse against her stomach. Her womb clenched at the prospect of being filled to the brim with every inch of this spectacular man.

His hands were everywhere, and she could feel her own arousal pushing higher to its peak. An inferno burned in his eyes. She felt beautiful, sexy, desirable. His fingers traced along both sides of her body. She arched to him, trying to position his cock against her entrance, but he swiveled his hips to move just barely away.

"Naughty girl. Not until I say so. You need to learn patience." He lifted a leg and swatted her ass.

Oh, God. *Naughty girl. Slut. Whore. You like it rough don't you. I'll show you rough.* Those words echoed in her mind, but with a sinister cast to the voice. Cal's voice. *No!* This wasn't Cal. This was Luc. She knew that in her head. So why wasn't her body listening? Luc raised her arms above her head, brought her hands together and pinned them down under one of his strong hands. Immovable. She couldn't control her breathing, the roar of blood rushed through her ears, and her vision blurred and black dots danced on the periphery.

"You're more delicious than I could've ever imagined. My cock is so hard for you, Avery. I can't wait any longer. I need to feel you come when I'm so deep inside you, you won't know where you stop and I begin."

Her entire body went rigid and she couldn't catch her breath. Fuck. Her eyes. She was scared to death. He halted every muscle in his body.

"Avery, beautiful girl, what's wrong?"

A scream made his blood run cold. He quickly released her hands, lifted his weight off her, and rolled to the side. She shot upright, pulled her knees to her chest, and started rocking.

"Avery," he tried to keep his voice as calm and soothing as possible, "it's me, Luc. I'm not going to hurt you. What's happening? Please talk to me." He couldn't make out what she was murmuring and her eyes had a glazed-over look that told him she was trapped inside a terrifying memory. It scared the hell out of him. He stroked her hair and whispered soothing sounds.

After a few minutes, her eyes focused on her surroundings and her shallow breathing became more regular. She looked at him. "Luc?" It was barely audible.

"Yes, Avery, it's Luc. You're safe, beautiful girl."

"Where am I?" She looked around the room, a bit dazed. Then it hit her. "Oh my God, Luc. I'm so, so sorry. I don't know what came over me. Please forgive me. It's not you. I swear it's not you."

Avery's eyes were as big as saucers. She avoided his gaze. The blush of embarrassment overtook her rosy glow of arousal. Shit. Something he'd said or did triggered a panic attack. He felt like the worst kind of dick. He knew he was on the brink of losing his shit. He never lost control. She brought out every primal urge he had from possessiveness to wanting to mark her as his like a goddamn caveman. This was more than simple lust from an intense scene. Avery meant something to him. She always did.

She leaped from the bed, swept up her clothes from the floor, and made a beeline for the bathroom. He had to make this right between them, couldn't let her retreat behind her walls. She needed to feel safe. He needed her to feel safe with him.

"Avery, stop," Luc commanded. She stopped before crossing the bathroom threshold but kept her back to Luc, shoulders slumped, chin on her chest and stood there trembling. Luc strode to her, allowed his chest and thighs to graze her back and legs, just to let her feel his non-threatening presence. She didn't move. He took that as a good sign and placed his hands on her hips to add an infinitesimal amount of pressure to hold her body to his. She could easily break his hold if she wanted to. Her body shuddered as she took in a deep, cleansing breath. Luc wanted to drop to his knees and give thanks when she let her clothes fall to the floor, placed her hands over his, and rolled her head back to lean on his shoulder.

"Shhhh, there is nothing to apologize for. You scared the hell out of me, but I'm here with you now. You're safe with me. I've got you."

He took one of her hands in his and led her back to the bed. He climbed onto it and sat with his back against the headboard and waited. Avery paused, warring emotions flitting back and forth in her eyes. Finally, she edged toward where he sat and allowed him to pull her onto his lap. Her heart was still thumping a staccato beat he could see and feel when she leaned against his chest. He pulled the sheet and blanket to cover them both and tucked it around her shoulders. He laid his arms outside the blankets, holding her gently without encasing her.

"It's OK now. It's just Avery and Luc. You're safe in my arms."

The trembling slowed only to be replaced by soundless sobs evidenced by warm tears trailing down his bare chest. He caressed her arms and back through the sheet while cradling her head against his chest.

Luc needed Avery to know he would never hurt her or force her to do anything she didn't want to do. Safe, sane, and consensual. He lived and breathed that creed. But this wasn't a negotiated scene. And Avery wasn't his sub. He didn't know enough about her hard and soft limits and her past to know what her triggers could be.

He'd fucked up.

Big time.

He could only hope she would allow him another chance to prove himself worthy of her submission. Hell, would she want to even see him again after this clusterfuck?

"I'm so embarrassed." Her ragged voice kicked him in the gut.

"Please, little one, please don't be embarrassed. I'm so sorry. Whatever I did or said must have triggered a painful memory. Please help me understand. If I know what I did wrong I can make sure I don't do it again. Would you do me the honor of sharing with me what you were feeling just before the panic set it? Can you talk about it?"

He gently kissed the top of her head and gave her a squeeze with his arms outside the blanket. He didn't want to frighten her any more than she was, but he knew she needed to deal with this episode if she was ever going to put the past behind her. Whatever that past was. Gryff's words echoed in his head about being gentle with her.

Avery curled into him and slipped her arms around his waist, took a deep breath and let it out. Her stiff muscles relaxed a bit and she sank into his hold. Elation ripped through Luc at the small but exponentially significant sign. That and their skin-on-skin contact did more to ease his jangled nerves than she could ever know. It felt so right to have her curled up in his lap, so natural. They just fit together. She kept her head buried into his chest, sighed, and started to speak.

"He used to tie me up."

"Your ex, Cal?"

"Yes. He would leave me like that for hours. Call me horrible names. Beat me."

"Ah, hell baby." Luc rocked them back and forth, trying to ease her pain.

"It didn't start that way. I guess it never does. I learned enough about Dominance and submission from Gryff and Marlowe to know I'm a sub. They were so patient with all my questions. I was planning on doing the training class, but I met Cal. I believed, maybe hoped, Cal was a Dom and I could learn from him. In the beginning, he was gentle and warm but pretty boring too. I could never seem to get wet enough for him which made him angry. He started to get rougher. At first, I liked it and my body responded. But it escalated insidiously. It got to the point where Cal controlled every aspect of my life and used force to strip me of all my power. The physical manifestation of his control was, relatively speaking, easy to deal with. Skin and bones heal in a finite period of time. But he was a master at humiliation. It was his words that wounded me to the core, not his fists. The vitriol in his voice oozed from every pore in his body.

"Cal was insanely jealous of my friendship with Gryff, though it was never anything more than that. He's like my big brother. Cal couldn't or wouldn't get that through his thick skull. When Cassie was two years old I found out I was pregnant with Cassie's brother or sister. There was no way I was going to bring another child into that environment. Gryff and I planned how I would tell Cal I was pregnant and was leaving him.

"The day came and Cal came home early from work in a rage. He saw our packed suitcases by the door and just lost it. He hit me across the face, in front of Cassie. I ran to the front door with her in my arms, hoping Gryff would be there. Because Cal got home about an hour early, Gryff hadn't yet arrived. Cal came up behind me just as I got to the front door. I put Cassie down and tried to move so Cal would follow me away from Cassie. He trapped me near the stairs to the basement and hit me again. I instinctively covered my belly rather than defend my face and he instantly knew. He called me a stupid bitch for getting pregnant again, claimed it couldn't be his kid, and punched me so hard in the stomach I couldn't breathe. I tried to catch my breath but lost my footing and fell down the basement stairs. The next thing I remember is waking up in the hospital with Gryff and my parents by my bed. I lost the baby."

Rage, sharp and unyielding, bubbled up inside Luc. He wanted to rip that bastard apart for what he'd done to this beautiful woman in front of her young daughter. But that was not what Avery needed. She deserved better from him. The hell she must have lived through. He shook his head in disbelief. Gryff had told him she had come a long way since Cal was locked up. Now he understood what his friend meant.

"Luc?"

"I'm here, beautiful girl."

"After all the hateful things Cal used to say to me, I thought I was finally at a place in my life where I could actually believe you when you call me that. Until about a half hour ago."

"You can believe it, Avery. You are beautiful. And sexy and smart and successful and incredibly courageous. I'm so very proud of you. You have a successful career, a beautiful daughter, friends. You should be proud of yourself. He never deserved you."

Avery took a deep breath and blew it out, relieving more of the tension she was holding in. Her body sank into his hold as she became lost in his fathomless dark eyes.

"I'm so sorry I lost control. My job as a Dom is to be attuned to your body, your signals both conscious and unconscious. I didn't protect you. I let my own needs and desires take over. Can you forgive me?"

"Please don't be sorry. There's nothing to forgive. I wanted you. I still want you, all of you. I know you're a Dom and I know what that means. I wanted to be ready to be the sub I know I am. I guess I still have some stuff to clear out first before I can be completely comfortable relinquishing control and not be afraid for my safety."

"Tell you what, you've had one hell of a day. Let me hold you. Let your body relax and just go to sleep. You're safe in my arms." Luc placed a finger over her lips so she couldn't object. "Shhhh. This isn't a race. We're not going to do anything you're not ready for. The D/s power exchange is forged through open, honest communication. This is how partners build trust, between each other and trust in themselves. We missed that step. And that's on me. Still, I learned a lot tonight about your needs and boundaries. I can be quite demanding. I will push you but not more than I think you can handle. It takes a strong woman to submit to a Dominant partner. Dominance isn't meant to take away that strength. I want to nurture it. Revel in it. Honor it. You're a strong woman, Avery. Once you believe that in your soul, you'll be able to effortlessly surrender to me. Then I'll take you to places you've never known, if you'll let me. Exquisite pleasure will be yours. You. Will. Be. Magnificent." Each word was punc- tuated with a sensual kiss along her jawline.

"I want to find that place, Luc. I'd like to find it with you."
Avery let out a big yawn. "I guess my body is ready to call it a
night. Thank you for your understanding and patience."

She burrowed into his side, pressing her cheek against his
thumping heart. What he wouldn't give to erase those horrible
memories from her body, from her heart. To make her unequivocally believe what an incredible creature she was.

For this woman he would be patient. His heart opened a
crack, enough to allow her brilliant energy to seep into the dark,
hidden spaces he'd planned on being buried forever. It was in her,
and he was just the Dom to tap into that inner light, that
resilience, that strength. He would coax it out from behind the
shadows of her past and nurture it so it would blossom to its
fullest expression. Yes, Luc knew what he needed to do.

"Come on, beautiful girl, let's get some sleep."

Luc moved down the bed so he was lying on his side, head on
his pillow. He pulled Avery with him, her back to his front, and
anchored her against him with his top arm. She let out a heavy
sigh and within minutes he could hear her deep, even breaths of
slumber. He nuzzled his face into the back of her neck, filling his
lungs with her delicate scent. He let out a contented sigh.

An hour later Luc was still awake. He watched her beautiful
face, calm and content in slumber, and kept replaying in his mind
what she told him about the night she left that son-of-a-bitch.
Warmth infused his chest knowing she felt safe in his arms, safe
enough to be able to have a little peace. Still, the torrent in his gut
churned.

He carefully pulled his arm out from under her and slowly got
up. She made the sweetest little sounds but stayed asleep. Luc
made his way downstairs to the family room, grabbed the pillow
and blanket from the end of the couch, and turned on Sports-
Center. He didn't like leaving Avery alone in his bed. But, he

didn't want his tossing and turning to disturb her. He was hoping she didn't notice he didn't sleep in the bed with her. With everything going on in her life how could Luc possibly explain that his nightmares were unpredictable, and he was afraid of waking her up with his screams? And on top of that, he was sure the last thing Avery wanted to hear was that he hadn't slept in an actual bed or with anyone since his wife died. Yep, that tidbit of information was best left unsaid. He hoped he could get at least a couple of hours of sleep then crawl back into bed next to her before she woke up.

13

Sometime in the middle of the night, Avery awoke to voices coming from downstairs. In a half-awake daze, she rolled over to reach for Luc. Instead she found cool sheets and a very big dog. Her first reaction was to panic because she was alone. Very quickly panic slipped into confusion. Rather than hide under the covers, she got up, wrapped herself in a robe that hung on the back of the bedroom door, and walked toward the voices.

She stopped at the top of the stairs and peeked around the corner into the family room. The TV gave off a soft glow, casting tendrils of light about the room. That was where the voices were coming from. Did they forget to turn off the TV? And where was Luc? Avery stopped midway down the stairs when she saw Luc asleep on the sofa, a bent arm covering his eyes. Her appreciative gaze swept over his muscular chest, down his well-defined six-pack to the tops of the notches pointing to hips that were partially hidden by a haphazardly thrown blanket. The sight of him stole her breath.

Her mind went back to hours earlier when those lips and

hands explored her body, eliciting sensations that would be seared into her memory for all time. She shivered as she remembered one of the orgasms that had ravaged her body.

Luc was a force of nature, and at the same time made her want to believe all the things he said about how beautiful and sexy she was. Even in high school he oozed raw power. She'd always been drawn to it. To him. He still had that aura, just now it inhabited him as a calm, controlled power that Cal never had. She now understood the difference even if Luc believed he lost control last night.

Avery opened herself to Luc in a way she rarely ever did. He soothed her, didn't condescend to her, made her feel safe. He seemed to understand the kind of emotional intimacy and physical touch she craved, though she didn't understand why he hadn't yet kissed her. On the lips. She wanted to believe their relationship took a big step forward when she'd opened up to him about her past. Hope flickered in her chest. Did Luc want a relationship with her? Did Avery want a relationship with him? Why hadn't he really kissed her?

Merlot trotted down the stairs, his big tail thumping her leg as he pushed by her. She already had a soft spot for the beautiful beast, but it grew even bigger when he plopped on the floor next to where Luc slept. Both let out a peaceful sigh when Luc reached down to touch the dog's head, content that their well-choreographed routine was complete.

Then it hit her. What the hell was he doing sleeping on the couch? He wasn't going anywhere. She was safe in his arms. Was it all BS? She spun and ran back upstairs and jumped back into bed. Her thoughts were a chaotic brew. Did he genuinely mean what he said, or was it all empty platitudes? Did her panic turn him off so much he couldn't stand sleeping in the same bed with her?

She was damaged goods. That was her reality. Why would an established, put-together guy like Luc want to have anything to do with someone with her past? Luc was a fantasy. Nothing more. The tears started again with that realization. How could she have been so stupid?

Dawn broke as Avery's tears finally relented and she fell into a shallow, exhausted sleep. She woke from the ensuite bathroom door opening and a wave of humidity billowing into the bedroom. Luc emerged with only a towel cinched at his waist and damp, tousled hair covering one eye like a marauder coming to pillage her. Even in her angry, confused state Luc was still the sexiest man she had ever known, and her body reacted accordingly.

"The bathroom is all yours, little one. Take your time. I'll go make some coffee and breakfast," Luc said in a considerate, if not a little affectionate, tone.

Avery hopped out of bed and ran into the bathroom, slamming the door behind her. She couldn't face him. What would she say? Do you prefer the couch to a bed? Why didn't you stay in bed with me? The last thing she wanted to do was pile onto the needy, fragile image Luc must already have of her. Anger and disappointment twisted the fist in her gut — directed at Luc or herself she couldn't say. Either way, it felt like shit.

Forty minutes later Avery walked into the kitchen to find Luc at the stove. Her heartbeat kicked up and her breathing became erratic as she stood next to him to fix herself a mug of coffee. Damn her traitorous body rendering her susceptible to his clean, musky scent and his sculpted physique. She was still hurt that he chose to not sleep with her, despite the words he placated her with. Not to mention she was still embarrassed about her panic attack.

Avery glanced up from stirring sugar into her cup to find him smoldering. She now knew the true meaning of that word. Oh man, sex on a stick. Just being near him sent her brain into a tizzy. Hunger stole across his gaze, not the pity she'd expected. The growing tent in the front of his pajama pants punctuated the surge of hormones flooding her body. She licked her suddenly dry lips, and an image flashed across her mind's eye of her on her knees, his hands wrapped in her hair keeping her head exactly where he wanted it, Luc's cock deep in her mouth. She tried to stifle a moan from escaping her throat.

"Good morning, beautiful girl? Are you hungry for…breakfast?" The smirk on his face said he knew exactly the images her depraved mind conjured, and he approved.

Embarrassment for panicking during sex, paired with arousal from the possibility of sex, cascaded a wave of heat through Avery that consumed the possibility of her playing the cool morning-after card. Great. She was thirty-eight years old going on eighteen based on her body's reaction to this man.

"Coffee is fine, thanks. I'm going to call Gryff to see what the plan is to get Cassie to school then I have to be at the office for an eight-thirty staff meeting."

She walked out of the kitchen into the living room with her cell phone, needing distance in order to get her brain firing on all cylinders. With a good plan for Cassie in place, she bolted upstairs, gathered her overnight bag, and headed for the garage door.

"Gryff says she's on the bus en route to school. He and one of his security buddies are meeting at my house to upgrade the alarm system. So, it looks like you won't need to babysit me tonight. Thank you for last night." She gave him a peck on the cheek, avoiding the eyes that would destroy her resolve to escape without further embarrassment.

Luc stepped in front of her, blocking the door. "Woah, woah, woah, little one. You can't just walk out of here like that."

Avery raised her hand, palm forward like a stop sign.

"It's OK, Luc. Really. I appreciate your friendship and how you helped me feel safe. It's over now and I need to get to the office. So, please step aside."

Luc didn't move. He peered down, tenderly placed his fingers under her chin, and tilted it up so she couldn't avoid his gaze. She did her best to conceal her confusion, hurt, and the fresh tears starting to form.

"I don't think what we have going on here is friendship." His low, melty voice was gentle but no less firm. She didn't know what to say. Luc sensed her confusion and moved out of her way. Avery took the opening and bolted for the door, jumped into her car, and threw the gear in reverse before the garage door lifted.

"I'll call you later."

Yeah right. How many women in how many countries over countless years had heard that line? "I'll call you later." What did that mean exactly? Later today? Tomorrow? Next week? Or was it a polite brush off? Avery couldn't believe he said it. Whatever. She had enough to worry about.

She backed out of the garage and headed toward the office. Determination buoyed her mood.

"Luc Christianson can bite me," she yelled to the universe.

Shit. That was not the image she needed to wipe the man from her memory banks. Avery reached for the power on the car's sound system. Led Zeppelin's "Immigrant Song" blared through her speakers. Damn it! That had been one of the songs Luc's high school band used to play back in the day. She couldn't hit the power off fast enough. Was everything going to remind her of Luc?

Avery arrived at the paper with her armor back in place. She didn't expect Luc to "call her later" so he couldn't disappoint her. He was a Dom and she wasn't ready to be a sub. That made the outcome of their time together inevitable. So why did it feel like she was losing something rare and precious?

Gryff channeled his inner rock star and brought his drumstick down on the final cymbal crash of "The Pretender" by Foo Fighters and the rest of the band expertly followed his lead.

"I knew you still had chops, brother."

Gryff's infectious smile warmed a corner of Luc's broken heart, still he hesitated. It had been years since Luc picked up a guitar. Not since he lost Sydney and Ella. Their death also meant the death of music in his soul. That part of himself that felt emotion, felt music, felt his heart beat, had all but shriveled up.

"It's been a long time, Gryff. You know that. I'm…very rusty."

"Come on, man. We all know what you've been through. It's time. You've been away from music for far too long. You need it to move on. You know it and we know it. Get off your lazy ass and prove to us you still got game."

Luc knew his best friend's goading tactics. His all-consuming grief had blocked out the piece of himself that heard and felt music. It used to be that he couldn't even handle the noise while driving. Lately, he noticed a shift deep inside. Gradual. Meaningful. Soulful. He craved music again. Curiosity about what was hitting the radio waves these days had him often reaching for the power button on his car's audio system. The other day he found himself humming "The Stage" by Avenged Sevenfold.

"All right, all right." Luc held up his hands in surrender, his Pelham Blue Gibson Firebird guitar still strapped to his body. "I still need a lot more practice before I'll be ready for the Canada Day gig. I can't have you guys showing me up in my own backyard."

Gryff jumped up from behind his drum kit to bump fists with Luc. "You've got this. You need this. The crowd's going to love it," Gryff said with a big grin.

Later that evening, after a couple more hours of working out the kinks, the guys packed up their gear and headed upstairs from Gryff's basement, which doubled as their rehearsal space.

"Thanks for letting me work out with you guys. And for your patience. I still have some work to do, but I'll be ready for next week."

"Don't worry about it, man. You've still got it. Besides, it's just a bit of fun. Not like we're getting paid. Right?" Zeke, the bass guitarist, chuckled.

"I know, I know." Luc held up his right hand like a stop sign. "It feels great to play. I'm looking forward to being on stage with you guys again."

And he meant it. Luc missed the rush of adrenaline that playing live in front of an audience gave him. Play, the kinky kind, was a rush, too, but it was short lived and lately more hollow. Music infused his soul with longing for a deeper connection to the world around him. One he had once thrived in.

Gryff closed the front door behind the other band members, turned to his friend and clapped him on the shoulder. "Stay for one more beer?"

Luc glanced at his watch and gave Gryff a quick nod. It wasn't that late. They headed to the kitchen. "Thanks again for getting me out tonight. It felt great to finger the frets again." Luc opened the fridge, grabbed a beer for himself, and handed another to Gryff.

"You've still got it, my brother. I knew you did. You just needed to work some shit out to clear the way for the groove to flow again. I wonder if our friend Avery has something to do with this awakening." Gryff smiled and waggled his eyebrows.

Luc couldn't hide or deny it, Gryff knew him too well. He looked up from the beer bottle that he'd absently picked the label off and smiled. "Yeah, I guess she does." That realization surprised Luc. He was even more surprised he admitted it out loud.

"Listen," Gryff said, "you know Avery's special to me. She's been a good friend for a long time. I've seen her through a hell of a lot. Been her shoulder to lean on and cry on. I'm not going to betray her confidence with the details, but let me just say that beneath that strong exterior is a wounded soul. She's come a long way, and I think she's ready to let someone in again. I see the chemistry between you hasn't changed despite the years. I think you could be good for each other. But, don't take this the wrong way, I will break your legs if you hurt her. If you're ready for something beyond a pick-up scene at The House then go for it. Just take it slow. Got it?" Gryff gave his friend the cop glare for emphasis.

Luc nodded thoughtfully, his gaze focused on the spot where his wedding ring used to be. "I hear you. It's not like I haven't had my share of heartache. You know that. You probably know both of us better than we know ourselves. This is the first time since… their deaths…that I've felt like wanting more than just a scene. She responded to me like a natural sub. It's intoxicating. She's intoxicating. For so long it's been as if I died in that crash along with my girls. But when I'm with Avery, it doesn't feel so dark and empty. Crazy, right?"

Gryff sighed like he debated sharing something. He leaned forward, rested his forearms on his knees, and clasped his hands together. "Let me just say this, she is a natural sub. I saw how she responded to you at the awards gala. But I also know someone in her past abused that sweet gift. She's not going to trust so easily again. Please, just be careful with her. That's all I ask."

He understood what Gryff was saying. Gryff had trained him to be Master Luc so he knew what made him tick, knew what he expected from his subs. Gryff also knew how he and Sydney played. They pushed each other's boundaries but never crossed the line of trust they worked hard at establishing, together. Playing brought them closer as a couple, focused their attention on each other, and strengthened their relationship.

After the accident, Luc's demands of his subs became harder, colder. The goal was hedonistic pleasure. For a few moments of bliss where the constant ache of loss disappeared into the ether of carnal release. But that was as far as it went. He played, they climaxed. Feelings weren't part of the equation.

"I get it, brother," Luc said. "She had a panic attack in my arms."

"What the fuck?" Gryff shot out of his chair to loom over Luc, hands fisted at his sides like he was seconds away from pounding his friend into the next room. "What did you do to trigger that?"

Luc's eyes must have telegraphed the sincerity of his remorse because Gryff took a calming breath and stood down, marginally.

"I had her wrists in my hand lightly pinned above her head. Just testing the waters a bit, you know."

Gryff glared and gave a single nod of acknowledgment. And waited for Luc to continue.

"I think something I said sent her back to that time in her life. As soon as I realized what happened I backed off and just held her. When she came back, she told me about her asshole ex."

"Motherfucker. Prison was too good for that cocksucker."

"Fucking right. She's a survivor, our Avery. I still can't fathom what he did to her and her unborn child. It's a fucking miracle she's as put together as she is."

Gryff sat back down and jammed his hands through his hair. "I regret that I didn't get them out sooner. I knew Cal was on the edge. I've seen the signs too many times from my days as a beat cop. We'd get the call from a distraught woman, arrive on the scene then she wouldn't press charges. The next time we saw her was either in emerg or the morgue. I refused to let Avery become another statistic."

"Thank God you were there for her then. Now she has both of us."

Gryff's eyebrows peaked. "Is that so?"

"Look, she's been our friend for years. Neither of us wants that fucker to hurt her or Cassie again."

"And…"

Luc nodded, squared his shoulders, and opened himself to Gryff's inquisitive glare before he spoke. "And, as you noted, we have incredible chemistry. She makes me want to feel again. When I think about Sydney and Ella it doesn't seem as if the pain in my chest is going to rip me apart. Something is changing inside me, and it's because of Avery. It's Avery I see in my head when I wake up in the morning. Christ, just thinking about tasting her again gets me hard. I want to see where this might go."

Avery was different. He wanted to get to know her, under-stand her, cherish her. And it felt good. The pain and longing in his heart where the emptiness lived started to ease. It was transforming into something peaceful and content. Could he be actually starting to heal from his shattering loss?

Relief swelled when Gryff's mouth curled up into the beginning of a smile. But worry still lingered in his eyes.

"OK. I'm thrilled you are starting to put the past behind you and look toward something positive in the future. I'm also glad Avery has you by her side. But you need to hear me on this. We both know Avery is a sub. She knows it too. That fucker led her down the proverbial path with promises of helping her find her submission. Instead she found abuse."

"I know what you're going to say."

"Do you? I think you could be good for her. You could train her. But only if you can take a step back and go at her pace, not the pace you've become accustomed to."

"I agree, on both counts. I see how she responds to me. Yet I triggered a panic attack. I need to earn her trust."

"That's just the beginning. Avery deserves the best. No one in her life has treated her with the respect and honor you bestowed on Syd. I think you can be the Dom Avery needs. The question is, will she let you?"

That was one question. The other rested with Luc. Could he be that Dom again? The one who took the time to unravel the woman to discover the sub in his arms. The one who cared enough about the woman to open himself up and allow her to invade his soul. The one who connected with his partner, strengthening their bond through D/s. The one willing to risk losing it all, again, in order to bask in the glow of her light for as long as she allowed it.

Luc stood in the middle of Gryff's kitchen, hands on his hips, and bent his head back to look up at the ceiling. "Sydney and Ella were my world. I miss them every damn day. A piece of my heart will always be theirs." His spine straightened and his chest rose as he looked to Gryff. "Avery lightens my heart. I feel myself smiling more than I have in years. Hell, I played my guitar tonight. That says a lot."

Gryff slapped his friend on the shoulder then pulled Luc in for a quick bro hug.

"You certainly look more alive than you have since they died. If Avery is the catalyst for you finding your way out of the dark hole you've been in for the past five years, then I'm happy for you my brother."

Luc's shoulders eased away from his ears. He hadn't realized how much his friend's approval meant to him.

"Thanks, man. I appreciate your vote of confidence."

"You have it." Gryff raised his hand and wagged a finger in Luc's face. "Just the same, I'm going to keep an eye on you both. If I see Avery unhappy or unsure of what's happening between you two, you will be answering to me. Am I clear?"

"You have my word."

Luc said good night and headed home.

Gryff's warning resonated. Luc understood his friend's protectiveness toward Avery. The same urge had flared to life when she sobbed in his arms. None of the other subs he'd played with since Syd ignited his primal need to protect. His first instinct was to lock her and Cassidy down somewhere safe until Gryff found the fucker scaring her with those messages. Luc snorted. He couldn't picture Avery acquiescing to that command. Hell, she fought against spending one night away from her home. Independence was a badge of honor she wore proudly. He would never want to take that from her.

Though images of her blonde hair wound around his fist, holding her exactly where he wanted her, obeying his command to not come as he pounded into her pussy from behind, had his cock straining for release from his jeans. Yes, Luc wanted to be the Dom who earned Avery's trust and her submission, but not at the expense of the woman she had become. That wasn't what the power exchange was about.

But, did this connection run deeper than just D/s? Luc rubbed his fist over his chest. Cracks were forming in the ramparts safeguarding his heart. Why didn't that scare the shit out of him?

15

Two days later, Avery still couldn't shake the confusion swarming her brain. She'd replayed the morning after her panic attack over in her mind so many times she wasn't sure the memories were real or figments of her overactive imagination.

The cool sheets next to her when she awoke were definitely real. Luc's compassion when she told him her story felt real. Or was wishful thinking overriding her logical brain? Maybe her sob story freaked Luc the hell out, but the gentleman in him made sure she settled down before he headed to the couch for the night. Who bloody well knew why he didn't sleep with her?

"Enough!" Avery shook her fists at the ceiling in frustration.

"Enough of what, girlfriend?" Rae bounded into Avery's office, plopped herself in one of the guest chairs on the other side of the desk, and crossed her legs, settling in for an extended stay.

"Nothing. Don't want to talk about it." Avery straightened a pile of neatly stacked papers on her desk then shook her mouse to bring her computer back to life, ignoring her friend's expectant stare.

"Right. It's definitely not nothing. You never bite anyone's head off, yet this morning you made that intern's lip wobble during the editorial meeting. Good on her for not letting a tear fall in front of everyone, but as soon as she made it to the ladies' room she let loose. Let's hope she doesn't quit. Who will you get to write the obits and notices? You seriously want to go back there?"

Avery flopped into her chair like her bones had disintegrated. "I hear you. You're right. I'm just trying to figure something out."

Rae enthusiastically rubbed her hands together and perched on the edge of her seat. "Oooh, a conundrum. Can I help?"

"How long have you been waiting to use that word in a sentence?" Avery's mood lightened as she couldn't help but smile at her friend's satisfied grin.

"Months. Now, spill it. What's got your knickers in a twist?"

Avery blew out a sigh. "Not what, who. Luc Christianson."

"What did that bastard do?"

"It's not like that, Rae. Or maybe it is. Hell, I don't know. That's the problem."

She told Rae what happened and what didn't happen because of her panic attack, and then how she woke up alone. Rae had been a supportive friend and a non-judgmental sounding board while Avery put the pieces of her life back together. She knew how to cut through the crap and tell Avery the truth, even if it hurt a bit. Kind of like a flu shot — a little pin prick in the short term for longer term protection.

A knock on her open door interrupted her story. The now-sheepish intern carried in a gorgeous bouquet of fresh cut flowers and placed the vase on the corner of her desk. Avery barely got out a thank you before the girl scampered out of her office.

When was the last time she had gotten flowers? It wasn't her birthday, and her promotion had been more than a month ago so that couldn't be the reason. Avery held her breath as she tore open the cello bag protecting the blooms and fished out the tiny envelope that held the card.

"What's it say? Who are they from?"

"How old are you anyway?" Avery marveled at her girlfriend's exuberance over just about everything in life. She seemed to vibrate with energy like a puppy who figured out how to wag its tail. All she needed to complete the picture were floppy ears and a slobbering tongue hanging out of the side of her mouth.

Avery avoided Rae's eyes, pulled the card and read it to herself and giggled.

Beautiful girl,
As wonderful as these smell,
they're nothing compared to your scent.
I can't wait to taste you again. Luc xo

Heat climbed her neck to her cheeks. Man, she hated when her body betrayed the polished, professional exterior she worked hard at honing. Moisture flooded her folds as she remembered how his tongue lapped at her relentlessly, sending her into another plane of existence with pleasure. The man had serious talent.

"Oh, now that's just rude. Throw me a frikin' bone here!" Rae said as she emphatically waved her hands toward herself, all with a big grin on her face.

"All right. They're from Luc."

"Does this mean he's out of the doghouse?"

"Maybe. I don't know. He gives me the best orgasms of my life then shuts down. He holds me while I ugly cry against his chest then can't stand to be in the same bed. Now he sends flowers with more than a hint about what he wants. What am I supposed to believe?"

"Bastard." Rae shook her head as she sank back down into her chair. "How dare he make you feel like the goddess you are, make you believe he cared about what you went through then leave you cold and alone while he catches up on the latest scores? Dirty rat bastard."

"Seriously." Avery blew out a heavy sigh. "Explain that to my raging hormones. I'm totally pissed at him, but you had to have been there, felt and saw how he looked at me, held me when I crumbled. He looked genuinely surprised when I left the next morning. Now these. I don't know what to think." Avery held her head in her hands, elbows propped on the edge of her desk. "We both need to get back to work. That will get me focused on something other than Luc Christianson."

"OK, I'll drop it for now. But, if he hurts you, I will personally kick his ass!"

"You'll have to get in line behind me," bellowed Gryff's alpha male cop voice. "Whose ass are we going to kick, Rae?" The corners of his mouth were curling up as he chuckled at the photographer.

Rae jumped up at the deep growl behind her. Amusement shined in Gryff's eyes. Rae peeled herself off the ceiling and punched him in the shoulder.

"Your dumbass buddy, Mr. Wineguy."

"Oh shit. What did Luc do?" Gryff said as he sat in Rae's chair without taking his gaze from Avery's face.

"Don't you have somewhere to be, work to do?" Avery glared at her girlfriend across the room.

"OK, boss, I'm going. But this little discussion between me and you," she wagged her finger back and forth between them, "isn't over by a long shot, sista." She spun on her heel and headed out of the office with a flourish. "Catch you later cop-boy."

"Not if I catch you first, babe."

Rae and Gryff flirted mercilessly, but they both knew it was all in fun. Gryff regarded Rae like he did Avery, a little sister and good friend. Gryff waved goodbye to Rae and refocused on Avery.

"What did I walk in on?"

No way would she discuss what happened with Luc's best friend. Plus, Gryff had witnessed enough of her ups and downs with Cal. She was determined to not lean on him like that anymore. Sure, she knew if she needed him, Gryff would be by her side before she could utter the request. This was about her pride. She could stand on her own two feet and get up on her hind legs if needed. Sometimes a girl just needed to vent to a girl-friend who would commiserate and not disclose where the bodies were buried.

"Nothing, girl stuff." Avery waved her hand dismissively in the air.

Gryff shook his head — he knew when she was hiding some-thing. Thankfully he also knew when not to push. "Whatever you say, doll. You know where to find me when you're ready to talk."

Avery sighed. "Yes, I know, thank you. I think I can handle this one. What brings you by?"

"Your new security system is all set to go. Are you about ready to call it a day? I can take you home and show you how it all works."

While she appreciated staying at her parents' house the past few nights, she was tired of their constant hovering. It was an omnipresent reminder of the threats and that Cal was out from behind bars, somewhere. That said, being back in her own home also meant being alone. Even though the new security system reassured her, she wasn't sure she would be able to sleep. She had to make sure Cassie didn't pick up on her fear. Her top priority was to make sure Cassie's world was as normal and happy as possible.

"Great. I have a few emails to return then I'll be ready to go. Do you mind hanging out for fifteen minutes or so?"

"No problem. I'll be back in a few." He got up and headed out of her office.

Turning back to her computer, Avery focused on a message from her crime reporter that outlined the latest updates on a local political corruption story. It seemed like he was making progress, still, Avery's gut told her there was more to the story. He wouldn't be happy, but she wasn't going to risk the paper's reputation, or hers, on a story that wasn't as accurate as it could be. That's what being city editor was all about. She just needed to suck it up and do what she knew was right.

Before she could click send, an email from Luc popped into her inbox. Her breath caught in her throat. What this man did to her. She tried to calm herself before clicking open the message. Avery didn't know what to make of this. It appeared like a blasted email advertising a Canada Day event at Sky Hill Winery. Then she saw it at the bottom:

Hope you and Cassie can join us.
My family will be there.
So will Gryff's. Bring your parents too.
Thinking about you. Luc xo

Avery liked the warmth that enveloped her. He was thinking about her. Ok. He earned a few more points but not quite enough to get out of her doghouse. Yet.

"That's the smile I like to see." Gryff stood in her office doorway, leaning against the frame.

Avery looked up and blushed. She didn't acknowledge his chuckle at her expense, just went about shutting down her computer, putting away multi-colored pens and a stapler, returning a stack of files to her cabinet, positioning her phone so it lined up with her monitor before shoving a few folders into her bag, satisfied that her office was go-home-ready.

"Let's go."

Avery's heart swelled with love for her daughter and her friend. As much as love surrounded her, for which she was eternally grateful, she knew something was missing. She wrapped her arms around herself, remembering how Luc comforted her. More than that, the desire brimming in his eyes had smoldered. Also there, in equal measure, was genuine caring and concern for her well-being.

Excitement supplanted anxiety as Avery considered the possibilities. Luc had invited her family to the Canada Day celebration at Sky Hill. He wouldn't have done that if he couldn't handle her past, or her present stalker for that matter. Could Luc be the Dom who would guide her on her submissive journey? Was she even ready to travel that path?

Lord knew Avery was attracted to Luc. That was the understatement of the year. He ignited an inferno she didn't know she was capable of experiencing. What a revelation. Now, that intense heat Luc unmasked was as necessary as air. She couldn't go through life and not feel that way again.

The word *yes* bubbled up from deep in her belly. She'd hidden behind her work, her daughter, and her past long enough. It was time to take a risk on her future. Her inner warrior goddess fist pumped her decision. But could Avery trust her to protect her self-respect? Would she be strong enough to walk away if Luc's behavior threatened her independence? Time to walk into her future.

16

The scent of fresh cut grass carried on a gentle breeze as Luc and his dad walked the grounds surrounding the winery, confirming the event was set up according to their specifications. Cicadas and bullfrogs competed for aural supremacy in the stand of trees bordering the vineyard. A bead of sweat tracked down Luc's back and the heat of the day was just beginning. Luc looked heavenward and quietly thanked his mom for arranging Mother Nature's cooperation on this important day.

Billy put his hand on his son's shoulder. "She would be so proud of you, son. How you've taken over here, like you were born to do the job."

Luc smiled at his dad. "Well, I guess I was after all."

It was a good day.

July 1, Canada Day, was always a happy occasion for the Christianson family and for everyone who worked at Sky Hill. Except last year — it was a somber reminder that Luc's mother, Maryse, had lost her battle with cancer only months before.

Billy and Maryse's love was one for the ages — powerful, true, and never-ending. The condo in Florida was supposed to be for their retirement. Together. Though Billy spent the coldest part of the winter down there to grieve and begin to heal from his unfathomable loss, Luc knew his dad couldn't retire from his life's work. Sky Hill was part of Billy's DNA. While Luc was now in charge of day-to-day operations of the company, he would always find ways to make his dad feel important, needed, and appreciated. Billy claimed he wanted to be on hand for the visitor season and harvest, just in case Luc or Gen needed him in this transition year. Or so he said. Maybe he needed to be back on the farm to feel connected to his late wife. And this annual celebration was a way to honor her loving memory.

Luc hoped Avery accepted his invitation to join the celebration and bring Cassie and her parents too. The weight of his own grief lightened when Avery smiled at him. Who was he kidding, he was excited to see Avery's beautiful eyes looking up at him when he revealed his surprise.

He normally wouldn't be that guy — big romantic gestures to sweep a woman off her feet. Hell, Master Luc only had to glare and nod his head to the floor to have a sub kneeling at his feet. But he didn't want any sub, he craved Avery. She was the one he wanted to claim, to proudly display his marks of ownership, to wear his collar. Desire flared hot. His fingertips pulsed, along with his cock, itching to caress her silky skin. Luc shoved his hands in his pockets in an attempt to hide his obvious arousal from his dad.

"Uh oh, here comes trouble." Billy chuckled and pointed toward the parking lot.

"With a capital T." Luc glanced at his watch and shouted to Gryff as he approached where they stood. "You're early. You know what that means. I'm putting you to work."

"Bring it on," Gryff playfully challenged with both hands waving toward himself and a boyish grin on his face.

"I'll leave you two boys to it. See you later." Billy headed off toward the winery.

Luc jumped at the chance to put his buddy to work. He helped the staff move the last few tables and chairs into place, lugged bags of ice to the portable wine bars out on the grass surrounding the stage and other manly tasks designed to keep him out of trouble. The girls on staff at the winery always swooned when Detective Gryffin Calder showed up and made it his personal mission to let them know in no uncertain terms how dazzling they each were. Man, the guy was smooth. Luc also knew how to make a woman swoon. Well, he used to.

Maybe it was time to flex those muscles again. Avery's eyes and body telegraphed how she felt about him. Desire burned bright, crowding out her irises and hardening her nipples to pebbles when he touched her, and she didn't try to hide it. Conversely, when she was pissed at him her stiff muscles flinched like she couldn't stand his touch. More than once over the past few days he'd wondered why she left him standing in the kitchen the other morning like she couldn't run out the door fast enough. What had changed from when she fell asleep in his arms? Had she still been embarrassed about her panic attack?

The thought of what that fucker did to Avery and Cassie made Luc want to pound the ever-loving shit out of him. Martial arts had taught Luc discipline and to use his skills in defense, not offense. But if he could get Cal alone, mano a mano, he would unleash every lesson he ever learned so the bastard could feel what repeated blows to the head and body actually felt like.

Avery's resilience, her independence, and determination to create a loving, stable home for her and Cassie was intoxicating. She didn't need him to take care of her. So. Fucking. Sexy. But this wasn't a simple case of lust. He wanted to earn Avery's trust and her respect so she would let him support her, stand by her side, catch her if she stumbled. Had she ever been able to rely on someone? Would she allow him to show her he could be that guy?

Luc and Sydney had forged a bond of trust creating the environment for Syd to flourish. That was what he wanted for Avery. With Avery. Could she trust any man after the hell she and Cassie had been through at the hands of her ex? Actions spoke. His actions had triggered a panic attack. He still felt like the biggest asshole on the planet for letting his control slip. He was better than that. Now he had to prove it to Avery.

A little girl's exuberant squeal pulled Luc's attention toward the parking lot. The sun's golden hue danced on Avery's soft, wavy tresses as they flowed behind her in the breeze. Her daughter held her hand though it seemed more like a tether anchoring the little pixie to the earth as her pink and green frilly skirt flounced with each leap and skip. Cassie's joy was infectious. Luc felt his cheeks bunch as a wide smile spread across his face the closer they got to where he stood, watching, waiting.

"Mommy, look at the bouncy castle! Can we go there first? I want to jump and jump and jump."

"Hold on there, sweet pea. First, we need to say hello to Luc and his family and thank him for inviting us. Then you can go bounce. OK?"

Cassie let out a defeated sounding, "Oh kay," while her grandparents both smiled.

"Uncle Gryff!" Cassie squealed with delight as she took off at full speed across the lawn to jump into Gryff's strong arms. Luc thought he heard a collective "aww" from the female staff when Gryff bent down, scooped Cassie up like she weighed nothing, hoisted her above his head with his arms outstretched, and spun them both in dizzying circles, all the while both of them giggling. Some big, badass Dom Gryff was now.

Luc could still feel Ella in his arms, hear her peals of laughter. Every molecule in his living form still held an emptiness that only Syd and Ella could fill. But the pain didn't consume him, rob him of his breath, like it used to. Instead, Cassie awakened a yearning for peace in his soul. He knew what it felt like to be filled with happiness. For his heart to be bursting with so much love for his girls he didn't think he could contain it.

The connection between Avery and Cassie shined brightly in their faces when they looked at each other. Unconditional love and trust flowed effortlessly between them. Luc missed being surrounded by that gift. He counted his blessings he had experienced that depth of love once in his life. Would it be selfish to ask the universe for another chance to experience that completeness, that bond with another person that supersedes all others, that place where acceptance of all of who he was freed him to breathe in everything life had to offer? The prospect of spending another five years going through the motions, separate from the surrounding world, scared the shit out of him. Maybe that was a good thing. He had expertly contained his emotions in a walled-up fortress he wasn't sure anyone could penetrate. But, these two had him wanting to try. That was something.

Luc's eyes locked with Avery's long before he was within speaking distance. His mouth watered in anticipation of tasting her again. Her mom's elbow jabbed into Avery's side as she whispered into her ear. Color bloomed in Avery's face, flushing deeper shades of red the closer he neared.

"Well, well. Luc Christianson. It's been ages since we've seen you." Avery's mother, Sheilagh Lewis, eagerly embraced Luc like a long-lost son before he had a chance to properly welcome Avery. "My, what a handsome man you've grown into." Avery's father just shook his head as Luc kissed both of Sheilagh's cheeks. "And so gallant too."

Luc, ever the gentleman, ramped up the charm with a broad smile and said, "Mrs. Lewis, you're as lovely as I remember." He offered his hand to Avery's father. "Mr. Lewis, welcome to Sky Hill. So glad you could join Avery and Cassie."

Avery's father met Luc's hand and gave it a vigorous pump. "Looks like you have a perfect day today, Luc. Is your father here too?"

"He sure is. I think he's still inside but will be out here any minute. Can I get you all a glass of wine?"

Luc took wine orders from her parents and quickly moved to where Avery stood. Before she could say or do anything, he took her elbow and pulled her close until daylight couldn't slip between them, bent down, and whispered in her ear. "I'm so glad you came today. You look beautiful."

She smelled divine. His lips brushed the soft spot behind her ear he knew would send shivers through her body. He couldn't help himself. Considering it was ninety degrees Fahrenheit and blazing sunshine, her visible tremble couldn't be mistaken for chills. He was grateful he could elicit that kind of reaction from her despite how wooden her muscles felt in his hands. He had some work to do.

Luc cautiously looked at Cassie then to Avery for approval. He understood the significance of meeting her daughter. Avery hesitated for a split second but acquiesced and gave a small nod. Relief surged through Luc. He wanted to show Avery with both his words and actions that both she and Cassie were safe with him. He could be their foundation. Someone Avery could count on for support. Someone she could trust with everything she was, including her daughter. He bent down to be on eye level with Cassie and gently took her hand in his. "Hi, Cassie. I'm Luc. I'm a friend of your mom's and Uncle Gryff's. Did you know that we all went to school together when we were kids?"

"Really? That must have been a hundred years ago!"

"Now, now, sweet pea, we're not that old." Everyone had a good chuckle at the precocious little girl's genuine astonishment.

"Nice to meet you, Luc," she spun to Gryff and in the same breath said, "can we go bounce now?"

Cassie and Gryff headed off toward the bouncy castle, hand in hand. Avery's parents followed the pair. Luc offered Avery a glass of wine and noticed a fine tremor in her arm as she took the stem from his hand.

"Thank you," she said without looking at him.

Luc cupped her delicate face with both his palms, not letting her gaze stray from his. "It's my pleasure, Avery. I'm sorry I have to leave you for a bit, but I have a few things to take care of. Please stay and enjoy the party. I'd like to spend some time with you later. Can you wait for me?"

Confusion flitted across Avery's gaze but she answered. "I'll try."

"That's all I ask." Luc bent and placed his lips on her jaw. "I'll see you soon."

Her eyes seared his back as he walked to where Gen stood next to the stage directing a couple of staff members.

Luc gave Gen a curt nod. Time to get his game face on. He mounted the steps to the stage and stood at the microphone.

"Hello everyone. My name is Luc Christianson and on behalf of my father, Billy, sisters, Geneviève and Anne-Sophie, as well as our extended family here at Sky Hill, we're delighted you're here to celebrate Canada's birthday with us. Canada Day was always a very special day in our family because it was the day our matriarch, Maryse, celebrated as the birth of her new life here in Canada. Though Mom is no longer with us, we feel her joie de vivre surrounding us. To get this party started we must have a little bubbly. It was Mom's favorite wine, not only for the taste but because of the pomp just from opening a bottle."

From behind a stack of speakers Luc pulled out a wickedly sharp looking saber, picked up a magnum of Sky Hill sparkling wine and with a single clean swipe down the shoulder slope of the bottle, popped off the crown, cork, and cage with as much flare and gusto as a swashbuckling hero proclaiming to save the fair maiden. The crowd erupted in cheers as the frothy wine erupted from the bottle filling a few flutes he had on stage.

Discretely, the Sky Hill staff circulated among the guests with trays of pre-poured sparkling wine so they could join Luc and his family in a toast. He paused long enough for the staff to reach all the guests then returned to the microphone.

"Now, if you can all raise your glass. To family, friends, and our incredible country where a woman from France and a local farmer found love and their life's work, together. May we all be as blessed as my mom and dad have been. Happy Canada Day!"

Everyone raised their glasses and took a sip of the bubbly pink wine.

"My mom believed in enjoying the moment. She also loved music of all kinds. This afternoon and evening we are pleased to bring you three amazingly talented local bands, each with their own style. Mom loved to dance. It didn't matter if it was the standards, pop, or even hard rock. If it had a groove she loved to move. Before the pros take the stage please indulge me and a few friends as we play for you." His bandmates took the stage and got situated with their instruments.

Luc continued as he slipped his guitar strap over his head and plugged into the amp. "We were very lucky kids because our parents were always supportive of our love of music, even while we were just learning how to play. We sure made a lot of noise back then."

The other band members nodded as laughter trickled through the crowd.

"Though none of us pursued music as a career, it continues to enrich our lives. Music, like wine, can be a soulful experience. When you discover a riff or song or a wine that moves you, it's magical. Avery, this is for you."

A very was chatting with a local mayor off to the side of the stage when she heard her name coming through the speakers. She faced the stage and looked up to see Luc smiling down at her. It was like they were teenagers, but this time Mr. Sexy Lead Guitarist was actually looking at her. At her! The familiar opening chords of AC/DC's "Back in Black" awakened her senses and without even realizing it, her body switched on and she began moving to the beat as effortlessly as twenty years ago.

Back in high school she went to all of their gigs. Everyone thought the boys in the band were cool — musicians and athletes and, of course, so very cute. All the popular, pretty girls would be at the front of the stage screaming for Luc, Gryff, and their buddies while Avery stood at the back of the crowd, her eyes glued to Luc. It didn't matter that there were four other guys on stage with him, she saw only him. She knew she didn't stand a chance with all the dyed blonde hair and pushed-up boobs being thrown at him. But that didn't stop her from imagining what it would have been like had they been together.

Half a dozen of her favorite rock songs later, Avery's neck was sore from her head bopping to the driving beat. She giggled at herself. When was the last time she'd enjoyed Canada Day this much? A couple of local grape growers were talking to her about the wet spring and the effect on local vineyards when she felt a familiar rush of tingles thrum through her body. Not that the conversation had had her undivided attention, but now she was completely distracted. Avery felt the crowd float away when she looked up and caught Luc's huge smile as he made a beeline for where she stood at the edge of the crowd. Lights flooded the stage, and the crowd cheered as the next band broke into their first song.

Then she heard his voice.

"Doug, Pat, thanks for coming by." Luc reached beyond Avery to shake their hands. "Can I refill your glasses? How about you, Avery? Another Sauvignon Blanc?"

Luc's hand at the small of her back felt like it was burning a hole through her shirt. It was delicious.

"Another glass would be lovely. Surprise me on the flavor."

Luc smiled and brushed his lips against her cheek as he excused himself. Was he staking his claim in front of these colleagues? No, couldn't be. He wasn't interested in a relationship with her. Hell, he couldn't stand to spend the night in the same bed as her. Yet, he just dedicated his band's set to her and was definitely acting all possessive in public. Maybe she was reading more into his actions than he intended. They were, after all, old friends. That must be it. She sighed, disappointment taking up residence in her gut.

Avery's head spun like some demonic character from the movies. She could hear her therapist's voice, echoed by Rae's — what do you want? That was a question Avery could easily answer. Luc. Always had, always would. But did Luc want her for more than a few D/s scenes? Would he give her a taste of blissful submission then pass her off to another Dom? Giving herself over to someone didn't hold the appeal it once did. Before Cal, the quest for the right Dom to trust with her body and mind preoccupied Avery's waking life. Cal effectively quashed that goal to the point that her independence from everyone was as necessary as breathing. Unfortunately, the cost of her independence was lonely nights with only her vibrator to warm her insides. Until Luc. He awoke the sub she'd tried to bury under layers of detached professionalism and busy motherhood. Submissive Avery was feisty and determined. And she liked this woman. Yep, three-hundred-and-sixty-degrees rotation.

The sun started to dip into the horizon casting broad swaths of purple, pink, and gold across the sky. The volume had been ratcheted up a few notches to party level, making conversation challenging unless you were yelling into someone's ear. But there were other ways to communicate.

Luc returned with fresh glasses of wine for them. After handing off the stems to his colleagues he turned to her and stepped forward until he was only inches from her, never dropping his gaze from hers. Gentle fingers slid along her jawline to push a wayward strand of hair behind her ear.

"So glad you waited."

His rumbling voice resonated along every nerve fiber in her body, alighting each like buzzing fireflies.

"Me too."

The smile that spread across his face didn't dampen the desire swirling in the depths of his molten eyes.

"Dance with me, beautiful girl."

Luc didn't wait for a response, not that it was posed as a question. He placed their wine glasses on the edge of the stage, grabbed both her hips and pulled so they were locked together.

His left hand took her right in a classic dance form. Then he rolled his hips, slipped his right hand to the middle of her back and gently rocked his fingers or the heel of his hand to urge her to follow. Rational thought evaporated into the sultry night air. They said more than fifty percent of communication was done through body language. Luc was a hell of a good communicator.

"Christ, Avery, what you do to me," he whispered in her ear.

Clearly, he wanted her. And that realization made her heart pound even harder against her ribs. What if she wanted more than just sex with Luc? OK, it wouldn't be just sex, it would be steamy, mind-blowing, earth-shattering sex. If she didn't have another panic attack. That was a big if.

Avery knew the kind of sex Luc liked. He wanted control. Dominance wasn't just a role for Luc, it was the underpinning of his thoughts, behaviors, actions. That was one of the reasons why she was drawn to him all those years ago. Back then, it was a wild heat that flared in his eyes and radiated off his body. Now it was an undercurrent of supreme confidence, not to the point of arrogance, just enough to be completely intoxicating. He would never hurt her physically, still she was petrified her body would betray her again. She couldn't survive that humiliation. Yet here he was, molded to her body better than her best-fitting shapewear, leaving no doubt about his arousal. Nor her own.

As the band progressed through their set, Avery relaxed and let her body move to the beat. It had been a long time since she saw a live band, but her body hadn't forgotten how to feel the groove. Though what she was feeling had more to do with the way Luc held her snugly against him, close enough that the ripples in his honed chest and abdomen rivaled the flutters in her belly. And the growing ridge between his legs told her he was enjoying this every bit as much as she was.

Luc overwhelmed her senses — blocked out the pounding

beat of the music, blinded her to the magnificently colorful sunset, shrouded the scent of fresh cut grass with his pheromone-laden spice. Could he honestly be interested in her as a woman? The very notion of her fantasy possibly coming true had her nipples hardening to the point of pain. Delicious pain that shot straight to the folds between her legs. Wasn't this what she craved? For Master Luc to whisk her away to another plane where her only job was to feel everything he bestowed upon her. That he would protect her, cherish her, and lavish her with untold pleasure. Yes, please!

The band must have finished their set because a breath of wind replaced Luc's solid wall of heat against her torso. And they had stopped dancing. She looked up at the stage and realized it was a completely different band from when she and Luc had started. When had that happened?

Avery was glad Cassie had gone home with her parents a couple of hours earlier. She had expended a lot of energy running around with Gryff and his brothers and even Luc. Avery's heart had filled with pride as she watched her little angel confidently chat with all the adults and make new friends with the other kids.

Cassie had been only two years old when Avery finally broke free from Cal's abuse, so she probably didn't remember anything. Every time Avery thought of the potential effects her bastard of an ex could have had on her precious little girl, she regretted staying in that house as long as she did. She lived with that guilt every day, probably always would.

"Why the solemn look, beautiful girl? I thought you were having a good time."

"Oh, it's nothing," she said with a dismissive wave of her hand, half a smile trying to curl her lips.

"That doesn't sound very convincing. Looks like the party is winding down and I'm all done down here. My dad and Gryff's mom are still catching up over a glass of wine inside the winery, so he'll lock up."

Luc picked up her purse from the grass next to her chair, pivoted toward the parking lot with a firm grip on her hand, and practically dragged her toward his car.

She could feel the intensity of his need sizzling through his hand where they were connected, yet he moved with the fluid grace of a panther on the hunt. She was his prey. That thought sent shivers down her spine and heat to her core.

They pulled out of the Sky Hill parking lot and headed around the corner of a vineyard block, away from Billy's house.

"Where are we going?"

"Patience, beautiful girl. I promise you won't be disappointed."

Avery knew she could take that promise all the way to the bank.

Luc pulled off the road onto a small access lane at the back of one of Sky Hill's vineyards. He popped the trunk to fetch a tote bag from the back and then made his way to open the passenger door and offered her his hand.

"Always the gentleman, Luc. You always make me feel special."

"It's easy when the lady I'm with is special."

It was a spectacular evening in Niagara. Cotton-ball clouds dotted the otherwise clear sky, setting the stage for hide-and-go-seek with the stars. A gentle breeze took the edge off the humidity of the day. The crescent moon hung in the sky like a character from one of Ella's favorite books. Luc was amazed at how the simplest things, at the most unexpected times, reminded him of his cherished daughter and wife. He resigned himself that they would always have a dedicated place in his heart. But lately, that place didn't seem as hollow and empty. Paired with a compelling need to bring Avery to this place, to show her this part of himself that hadn't seen the light of day for five years, drove Luc to plan this private vineyard tour. A whisper of peace fluttered in his chest. Curious, but not altogether unwelcome.

Avery didn't say a word but her tight grip on his hand and her shallow, rapid breaths revealed she was either nervous or on her way to being excited. Maybe a bit of both. He could work with that.

"Almost there, little one. Don't worry, I've got you," Luc said with a reassuring squeeze of her hand.

"Almost where, Luc? Oh, why are there no vines in this block?"

"That's what I wanted to show you," Luc replied and tugged her toward him, needing the feel of her body against his, rooting him to this piece of earth at this moment in time. Her unique scent mingled with the familiar — soil, grass, Mother Nature. *Home.*

He pulled a blanket out of the tote bag and spread it out on a patch of grass with the flourish of a matador, sat down, and extended his hand to invite her to join him. She slipped her fine-spun hand into his, dipped into a curtsy, and allowed him to guide her to the blanket. The schoolgirl giggle she tried to smother behind her hand was delightful. He couldn't resist tucking a wayward lock of her silky hair behind her ear. She sighed and let her cheek melt into his palm.

Luc reached back into the bag and pulled out a bottle of wine, two stemless wine glasses, a small charcuterie board protected with plastic wrap, a corkscrew, and two linen napkins. An extra pair of hands would've come in handy. One pair to never let go of this woman, the other pair to lay the world at her feet.

"You never cease to amaze me, Luc Christianson."

"And you're good for my fragile ego, Avery Lewis. Can I pour you a glass of our 2010 'Old Vines' Pinot Noir?"

Avery snorted. "Fragile ego my ass! Did I ever tell you that Pinot is my favorite grape variety?"

Luc chuckled. "I may have heard that once before. Why do you love Pinot?"

Avery lay back on the blanket with her hands behind her head and gazed at the night sky while starlight danced on her ivory skin.

"Lots of reasons I guess. I don't mean to quote *Sideways* here, but this is what I honestly believe. It's the viticulturist's grape. You have to be meticulous in the vineyard, all season long, and even then, if Mother Nature doesn't cooperate just so, you could end up with boring wine. If the winemaker can have a gentle hand in the cellar, Pinot can be so expressive of the place where it's grown. Here in Niagara we can grow Pinot Noir every bit as wonderful as some of the top sites in Burgundy. In particular right here on the St. David's Bench, where yours is grown. Here in the silty clay loam soil the wines develop an earthy quality that just floors me. And in the top vintages, the strawberry and raspberry notes add a layer of freshness. I love that each time you take a sip you discover another layer. It's not in your face like a Cabernet Sauvignon, but it can be every bit as age-worthy and food friendly. Pinot is beguiling like a sexy woman — enticing and pretty on the surface with a solid backbone made to stand up to the most complex dishes. Yet, it's soft enough to enjoy sipping on its own with a good friend on a starry night."

She looked up at Luc and smiled with a tenderness and strength that punched him in the gut. She got it. She fucking got it. He was mesmerized.

"I'm speechless. No wonder you're the writer and I'm the dumb jock who needed an English tutor."

"Whatever," Avery said with a playful punch to his shoulder. "You can't play that role with me, mister. I know better. You were a successful Bay Street corporate lawyer. You can't be dumb and make it to partner like you did."

Luc feigned pain in his shoulder where she'd hit him, rubbing it and giving her a rare hearty laugh. "OK, OK, you got me there. But it worked when I wanted the prettiest girl in high school to tutor me in English, didn't it?"

"You think you're so smart now? Are you going to open that bottle or just tease me with it?"

"Darlin', I don't tease. Unless I think you need to be teased."

An overwhelming need to kiss her, bind her to him in such an intimate way drove him to connect. Pure, carnal instinct fueled his craving to claim her as his own. That need vanquished his guilt and compelled his body to do what it ached to do every time he thought of his Avery. He couldn't hold himself back any more than the relentless pounding of waves on the shore could cease on command.

Luc bent down, cupped the back of her head in his palm, and gently pressed his lips to hers, their eyes locked together. He wanted to devour her but knew she needed to come to him on her own terms. He couldn't lose control like he did the last time they were together. She deserved a man, not a horny teenager who couldn't keep his shit together. She needed to be cherished, savored, honored.

Then, Avery took control of the kiss, shaped it, heated it, demanded it. She threaded her fingers through his thick, wavy hair and pulled him down on top her. Her tongue flicked at his lips, asking for entry, which he eagerly obliged.

He took her lead and plunged into her mouth, dueled with her tongue, reveled in every breath and taste. Sensuous purrs emanated from her throat, fueling his raging hard-on to the point of pain. God, she was delicious. He pulled back without losing contact and was floored by the flames he saw in her eyes.

"Can you let me take control, beautiful girl? I promise to take good care of you."

She arched into his body. "Yes, Sir. I would like that very much."

He ground his leaden cock into her pelvis, letting her know how much she lit him up. He slipped one hand under her hair and squeezed her nape. Not to the point of discomfort, just enough to let her know he accepted and appreciated her acquiescence. Her body bowed up into his. He filled the gap between her back and the blanket with his other hand, anchoring her to him, and rolled them so she was on top. Her pelvis locked into the cradle of his like the perfect key filled its mated lock. His cock pulsed in response to her hips rocking to find the spots where their notches lined up. Gold-spun hair shined in the moonlight as it cascaded over her shoulders forming a silken curtain that blocked out the rest of the world. It was just Luc and his beautiful girl.

He looked up, and her gaze captured his. Deep in those fathomless pools of sky blue he saw a different woman. Gone was the fear that supplanted every other emotion. Instead what he saw was a sexy, sultry, relaxed Avery who appeared to be completely at ease with him. A woman who owned her sensuality and wasn't afraid to bare it to him. He liked that look on her face. A lot.

Luc slid his palm along her shoulder, up her neck, wrapped his hand with the golden strands and gently tugged. Her eyes darkened with smoldering desire the moment her scalp prickled with pinpoints of pleasure-pain. Surprise and understanding swept across her face. Her rose bud lips parted on a gasp, leaving her mouth open to his invasion.

Luc took her mouth like a man possessed. His tongue easily

slipped past her teeth as she met him stroke for stroke. There was nothing tentative about this kiss. She inhaled him, giving as good as she got. All the while gyrating her hips like she was riding him in the Kentucky Derby. And those sexy little sounds she made had him so close to the edge he prayed he didn't blow right in his jeans. Control. He needed to keep a tight lid on his intensity. He couldn't overwhelm her again. *Time for a breather.*

She let out a disappointed growl when he pulled his head back, breaking the connection with a soft pop, and rolled them so they were seated facing each other. He avoided her heated gaze and grabbed the corkscrew and bottle of wine, giving himself a moment to summon Master Luc's control.

"How about that glass of wine I promised?" Luc's voice sounded as if his vocal chords had been through the crusher-destemmer.

"I think you're teasing me." The corners of her swollen lips curled up into a sexy-as-hell half-smile.

All he could do was groan. Her breathless voice told him she wasn't unaffected either.

Luc made quick work of the capsule and cork, poured a small amount of wine into his glass, and brought it to his nose. Once he confirmed this was indeed a good bottle, he poured Avery several ounces of the aromatic red nectar into the other glass and handed it to her. "I hope this bottle matches your eloquent description."

"I've had this wine before so I know it's wonderful. But, I thought you were long sold out of this vintage. Thank you for this special treat."

"Stick with me, little girl, and I can find more where this one came from," Luc said with a mischievous waggle of his eyebrows.

A grateful grin stretched her delectable lips as she took the stemless glass from his hand, lingering long enough for them both to feel the sparks arc between their fingers. He watched in awe as Avery closed her eyes, lifted the glass to her nose, and inhaled deeply, letting the aromas envelop her senses. She was so beautiful in the moonlight, honoring his family's wine with such reverence and care. His eyes were transfixed on her succulent lips as they parted just enough for her to place a small amount of the wine in her mouth. She held it, sucked in a little air, rolled it around with her tongue and swallowed, throwing her head back, exposing her elegant neck. He didn't think it was possible, but he got harder, making it uncomfortable to sit.

"Mmmm. Even better than I remembered."

Luc was gobsmacked. Now who was teasing whom? He was thankful his muscle memory was able to pour himself a glass and take a sip without wearing half the contents of the bottle.

"You never did answer my question about why this block isn't planted."

He half chuckled, half growled, his nose grazing the indent behind her ear to release more of her mouthwatering scent. "That's because you distracted me."

"Oh, well, that was purely intentional."

Luc took Avery's glass and placed it beside his on the blanket, palmed her hips, and pulled her back between his legs, leaning her back against his chest so they could both enjoy the night sky. Their bodies nestled together like staves of an oak barrel — they more than just fit, they were meant to snug together to give each other impenetrable strength.

D/s required trust. Not just physical but also emotional. Avery had opened herself to his scrutiny, but he hadn't allowed her the same courtesy in return. If he wanted to explore this growing connection between them, he needed to lay bare his soul. Get it all out there so she knew exactly why he'd been a cold bastard for the past five years. And why she was the only one who threatened to smash to smithereens the fortress of ice he had built surrounding his heart. *It was time.*

He handed the glass back to her and began.

"When Mom and Dad planted this vineyard, they left three open blocks back here away from the winery, tucked up against the Niagara Escarpment. One was for their home, one for me, and one for Gen. Sophie would get their house when they retired to Florida."

"That sounds so wonderful Luc — all of you living close to each other yet still having your own space."

"That's what they wanted, and we did too. Still do. We each went off to explore our own lives, make careers for ourselves, always knowing there was a place to come home to."

"Your mom and dad built their home so why not you and Gen?"

Luc closed his eyes, took a fortifying breath, and continued. "I was ready to make a move out of Toronto soon after Ella was born. I wanted to raise her in my family's way of life, not in the concrete jungle and monster homes in Toronto's subdivisions. Syd went along with the initial stages of meeting with architects and designing her dream home. After a few months it was obvious she'd either had a change of heart or was never sold on the idea of moving here in the first place. I figured that if we just kept going with the planning she would get into the process and fall in love with the idea. I was wrong."

Avery stroked his calf, quietly reassuring Luc he was safe with her, like she was safe with him.

"We argued about it constantly. She wasn't prepared to give up practicing law, and she couldn't believe I was willing to walk away from my firm when it was clear I was on the partner track. Truth is, I was getting more and more disillusioned with the whole corporate law scene. Too much posturing, too many fake smiles, way too much money being thrown about with little care for the people involved. I wanted to come back to my roots. Literally and figuratively. The day of the accident, I was on the phone with them as it happened. I was in the office trying to close yet another deal."

Luc could feel the tears pricking the back of his eyes. Avery slid her arms over his, encircling her waist and squeezed, compelling him to continue.

"I was supposed to go to Barrie with the girls to see Syd's parents. We argued big time, and I used work as an excuse to beg off on the trip. I just needed some time alone. Now that I'm home I know it was the right move for me. I'm happier here in Niagara, at Sky Hill, rather than in Toronto at my old firm. What does that say about me and my relationship with my family? What if the accident never happened? Would we have moved down here? I'm not so sure. Sometimes I wish I had been driving that day so I would have died with them."

Avery gasped and spun so she was kneeling between his legs, her eyes level with his. She grabbed his face between her hands and forced him to meet her gaze.

"Don't you dare say that, Luc."

The conviction in her voice astonished him. His vision tilted as Avery pillowed his head on her chest. Warmth seeped into his body from each point where they touched. He didn't deserve her tenderness. That was when the dam broke. Luc couldn't control his tears.

It's my fault I'm still here and they're not.

18

"It's getting late and you probably have to work tomorrow. I'm sorry for dumping my shit on you. I don't know what came over me."

Luc wiped his face with a napkin, stood, and gathered their things. Master Luc had returned — cool, aloof, in control. Distant. Avery's head spun like she was on a carnival ride, unable to lock onto solid ground while her surroundings whooshed by in a blur. The man went from all but inhaling her, to sharing his deepest wounds, to shutting her out in less time than it took to finish a glass of wine. Did he think she would turn away from him or pity him? She needed to shut that shit down now.

Avery not-too-gently palmed both sides of his face and lifted his head so he could see her fury. "Don't you dare blame yourself for a freak act of God! It was snowing. They lost control and got caught in a multi-car pileup. What you're feeling is survivor's guilt. You're a good man, Luc Christianson. You need to let it go. Savor the good memories and move forward. Build your dream home. Honor them but live for you."

Luc's lips appeared to be glued together, but she wasn't sure if he was fighting to keep words in or straining to get them out. Guilt still swirled in his eyes as his internal battle for control over his emotions furiously waged. But he didn't discount what she'd said. That was something.

The guitar strum ringtone of Luc's cell phone broke the heavy silence that sat between them.

"Hey, Dad. What's up?"

Avery watched Luc's face with concern as his eyes shifted and filled with worry and his eyebrows slashed low on his forehead.

"No, I haven't seen Merlot. I'm around the corner at the open blocks. I'll make my way back to your house and look for him on the way."

Luc helped Avery up from the blanket and relayed his conversation to her. His dad had arrived home with their German shepherd, Merlot, nowhere to be found. Normally the gregarious dog was an enthusiastic welcoming committee or ferocious guard dog, depending on who approached the house. Tonight, he was conspicuously absent. Even his dad's repeated calls didn't bring his faithful companion bounding to his side. His dad was rightfully concerned.

They jumped into Luc's car and slowly made their way toward his dad's home, careful to scan the sides of the roads. Dogs and cats were notoriously vulnerable to speeding cars on these dark and fast country roads, not to mention the packs of coyotes always on the prowl, though a coyote attack on a strong, large dog like Merlot would be very unlikely.

As Luc turned the car in to the long driveway leading to his father's home, the headlights illuminated something lying at the edge of the lawn, half in the drainage ditch that ran alongside all the rural roads in the region. Luc angled the car to point the headlights toward the object, and Merlot's face came into view.

Avery instantly knew something was wrong. She had her car

door open before Luc slammed the gear into park. She took off running toward the limp form.

"We found him!"

Avery heard Luc's voice and his footfalls running up behind her where she knelt next to Merlot's head. Still with his phone to his ear Luc bent down to feel for a heartbeat under the dog's front leg while she put her face next to the dog's nose, praying she could catch a wisp of a breath against her cheek.

"He's breathing!" Avery exclaimed.

"Dad, hang up and call Tom Martin. Tell him we're heading to the clinic and for him to meet us there. No, it's OK, you stay there, and I'll call you as soon as I get any news."

Luc shoved his phone back into his pocket and ran his hands over Merlot's body checking for signs of major injuries. There was no blood on the grass, but it was better to be extra cautious in case he had internal injuries. When his hands showed nothing obvious he cautiously wedged his strong arms under the dog to cradle him against his chest.

"Easy buddy. You're OK now. I'm going to get you to your friend Doctor Tom and he'll fix you right up. Everything is going to be fine."

Avery's heart was in her throat. The last time she saw this beautiful animal he was the picture of health, now Merlot looked like a rag doll. His breathing was labored and he used every last bit of energy to look up at Luc with sad eyes as if to say, "help me," and drag his tongue across Luc's chin. A tear left a salty trail down Avery's cheek.

"I'll drive." Avery didn't wait for Luc to agree. "You get in the back with Merlot. Cradle him in your arms to try to stabilize his body and keep him as still as possible. He'll draw strength from you."

Luc hesitated for a split second. She gave her head a terse nod to let him know her directive was not a suggestion. The keys were still in the ignition and the car running so she opened the passenger door, pushed the seat forward and helped guide Luc and Merlot into the small back seat. Luc may be a Dom, but Avery was a mama bear when someone she cared about was hurt.

They pulled into the vet's parking lot just as the lights inside the small building came on. Avery stopped right in front of the main door, shoved the gear into park, turned off the ignition, and leapt out of her seat before Luc popped the passenger seat out of his way. Together they entered the clinic and handed off Merlot to the vet and his assistant who were awaiting them. As the gurney rolled through the doors leading to the treatment area the sweet dog lifted his head and looked to Luc with what could only be described as thanks. Silent tears streamed down Luc's face.

Avery's heart broke for this beautiful man. First, he shared how he wished he was in the car with his wife and daughter when they died, then he found his family's dog seemingly near death. She took his fur-covered hands, led him to the waiting area, and guided his muscular body into an uncomfortable plastic chair. She tried to sit next to him, instead he pulled her down onto his lap and curled his body into hers. An occasional hitch in his breath from silent sobs was the only movement his wooden form allowed. Avery wrapped her arms around his neck and held on, held him while he waited, held him as he rebuilt his armor.

It could've been minutes or hours, Avery wasn't sure, when the doors to the treatment area finally swung open. Luc latched onto her hand, his grip telegraphing his concern for his buddy and his thanks for her support.

"Do you know where Merlot could have gotten a large quantity of acetaminophen?" the vet asked with both anger and concern lacing his voice.

Luc was taken aback. "Acetaminophen? How could he have eaten pain medication?"

"That's what I'm asking. The blood work shows Merlot is suffering from acetaminophen poisoning."

Avery watched, helpless, as Luc tried to process the news. He paced, ran his hands through his hair, cursed more than she had ever heard from him before.

"Tom, you know my dad is a responsible pet owner. He would never leave medication accessible to Merlot, or anything harmful to pets for that matter. You've known our family for decades. You know this."

Luc's terse response forced the vet's shoulders to drop a few inches. Both men stood down from their righteous stance, recognizing love for sweet Merlot in each other.

"You're right, Luc. But I had to ask. Merlot's been otherwise healthy. He's a strong dog. We just need to flush his system and he'll be OK. I'm not sure how much he ingested so we're also going to administer activated charcoal to see if we can stop any more from entering his bloodstream from his digestive tract. He's going to need around-the-clock care for a few days to make sure his body doesn't have any reactions to either the acetaminophen or the medication we gave him to counter the poison. We also need to closely monitor his liver to make sure there's no permanent damage. Do you want me to call your dad and let him know?"

"No, I'll tell him." Luc shook the doctor's hand. "Thank you for everything, Tom. We know our boy is in good hands."

Luc pulled out his phone as soon as the vet returned to the treatment area. Avery figured he would want some privacy, so she headed for the door. Fresh air would help her sift through the barrage of thoughts screaming in her head. She didn't make it to the door before a muscled arm banded around her waist and hauled her backward into a solid wall of muscle.

"Please."

She barely heard the plea. But she did feel the tension uncoil in Luc's chest as he held her, back-to-chest, and rested his forehead on her shoulder as if its weight was unbearable. She knew how that felt.

Warmth spread behind her breastbone. Luc needed her. Needed her strength. Needed her to be his solid ground. Other than Cassie, no one had ever leaned on her. Resolve fortified her spine, strengthened her resilience, bolstered her bravery. She could be the woman Luc needed. For now.

Avery placed her hand over Luc's and stroked the back of his hand with her thumb in a cadence that reminded her of Cassie's favorite Gaelic lullabies Closing her eyes, she focused on bringing her breathing and heartbeat into sync with the gentle rhythm.

"I know, Dad. I'm just as shocked as you are. How the hell did he get enough acetaminophen to cause this?"

Luc paused, listening to his father over the phone, his chest rising and falling in shallow, stiff, staccato beats.

"No, Tom knows we wouldn't leave anything harmful where Merlot could get into it."

His arm anchored her tightly against his side as if she was his lifeline and he dared not let go.

"He's got to stay here at Tom's for a few days. He's hooked up to an IV to flush the crap out of his system. They need to watch him closely in case he has a bad reaction to the medicine. The next twenty-four hours will be critical to see how he'll respond."

Luc finished the call and shoved his phone in his jeans pocket. Anger whipped through his body, hardening each muscle like drying concrete. Avery forced her body to remain supple, soft to his hard, calm to his turmoil, quiet to his dissonance. Words between them were redundant.

Patiently, she stood there. Her body recited a monologue worthy of any Shakespearean tragedy — hopeful Luc heard every word.

Slowly, Luc's breathing fell in lockstep with hers. Each inhale and exhale were purposeful cycles of cathartic release.

Gradually, tension in his body dissolved. Shoulders, pecs, abs, biceps each relinquished their excess energy back into the ether.

Luc stood to his full height, spun her in his arms, and gifted her with eyes that were wide open. For her. In their depths she saw vulnerability and in equal measure determination.

Avery palmed his rugged jaw, stubble prickling her fingertips. A gentle smile tugged at the corners of her lips. "Thank you for trusting me enough to be here for you and to allow me to see another side of the man you have become. I'm also thankful Merlot is getting the care he needs and hopefully he is on the road to a speedy and full recovery."

"I'm so grateful we found him and not my dad, so he didn't have to see Merlot lying by the ditch like that. I'm not sure he could handle losing his sidekick so soon after losing my mom."

"You're a good son, Luc. I'm sure your dad appreciates having you back home, so he can lean on your broad, strong shoulders."

Luc rubbed the back of his neck, exhaustion evident in his face. It had been a night of heavy emotions — from sharing his guilt about the car accident that claimed his wife and daughter to rushing his four-legged family member to the vet only to learn the dog had been poisoned.

"My shoulders don't feel all that strong at the moment. But you, beautiful girl, were a rock. I can't thank you enough for staying here with me. You must be exhausted. Let's get you back to your car."

Gentle lips along her jawline punctuated Luc's words of thanks. Warmth infused her muscles and bones and veins. This man. Even though he had to be still processing what happened with Merlot, layered on top of the ragged edges left behind from his outpouring, he still soothed her. Was concerned about her. Needed to take care of her. It was a thoughtfulness born out of caring about each other for many years, not a stifling possessiveness that threatened to eradicate who she had become. And, in equal measure, Luc was man enough to allow her to be the lifeline he depended upon to guide them to a safe haven. Give and take. Complimentary moments in time. Reciprocal sharing of burdens. All foreign concepts in her former marriage, yet oddly befitting with this man.

19

L uc needed to change the subject away from his so-called strong shoulders. He certainly didn't feel like that guy she'd just described after breaking down in front of her like a blithering idiot. Master Luc didn't lose his shit. Master Luc was solid. This was exactly why he shut himself down. Why he only played with subs once. Feeling meant all the guilt and grief would bubble to the surface again like a geyser about to blow. Tonight, he peered into the abyss that was his heart to let Avery get a glimpse of the darkness that had invaded every inch, her compassion scratched the surface and he blew like Old Faithful. Then, seeing his dad's devoted companion lying helpless in the ditch crushed him.

He didn't deserve her compassion or forgiveness. Yet he longed for it, ached to feel whole again. Avery's strength was an unexpected and welcome gift. No doubt she was still healing from the trauma she'd endured at the hands of her fucker of an ex-husband. Some people never completely put that kind of crap behind them. But the way she took control, without hesitation, when they found Merlot was totally badass. She was strong enough to let Luc drop his he-man walls to exorcise some of the demons festering in his soul. Avery stood by his side while he crumbled. Didn't flinch. Didn't wither. Didn't bolt. He was exhausted but felt lighter than he had in years.

Shafts of warm oranges and yellows blazed across the sky casting Sky Hill's vineyards in morning light. Dawn. New beginnings. Dark circles had appeared under her eyes from being up all night but to him, in that moment, she was simply stunning. Tenderness, strength, and something else he couldn't or didn't want to name glowed from within her sky-blue eyes, turning them an iridescent, clear blue, like precious gems that captured the light surrounding them.

Avery infused his soul with purpose. What was it about this woman that made him begin to feel again? He needed to matter to someone again. And, he wanted to be the man Avery needed.

The hair on the back of Luc's neck started to tingle. Avery's car was the lone vehicle in the parking lot. As they pulled up next to it, Luc's attention was caught by something stuck under her windshield wiper.

Luc grabbed Avery's forearm. "Stay in the car. Call Gryff and tell him to get over here, now." The command came out curter than he intended, but he was in full Dom protective mode in a heartbeat.

Luc reached for his door handle and cautiously got out of the car as he scanned the parking lot and beyond. He closed the gap between the cars in two strides. It was a blackened, dead Stargazer lily with a gooey, red liquid oozing down the windshield. Another note flapped in the breeze, trapped under the windshield wiper.

The dog was lucky.
Next time you won't be.

It looked just like the note left in Avery's purse inside the winery. He pulled out his phone, took a picture, and sent it to Gryff. His friend didn't waste any time calling back.

"Yeah, it's Avery's car. It's in the parking lot at the winery. Fucking prick." Luc didn't try to hide his anger and frustration from Gryff.

"I'm en route. ETA ten minutes. I'll alert forensics. Don't touch anything. Get in your car and move away but keep her car in sight."

"Got it."

Luc jumped back into the driver's seat, sped to the loading dock of the winery to tuck his car behind some semblance of protection while still keeping her car in view.

He looked over to Avery. Her face had drained of all color, her hands clasped so tightly together the knuckles were white, and her eyes blankly stared out the windshield.

"It's another message, isn't it?"

The monotone of her voice barely concealed the cauldron of emotions brewing inside her stock-still body. *Shit.* She had that remote, depersonalized look like just before another panic attack. Could he keep her grounded in the present?

The click and whirl of the retracting seatbelt echoed inside the car. Luc slipped his hands under her thighs and behind her shoulders and pulled her across the console into the cradle of his lap.

"Yes, beautiful girl, it is. Gryff and the forensics team will be here any minute. I've got you. Breathe with me. You're safe in my arms."

He gently swiveled her head so she faced him. Fear, raw and jagged, had taken up residence in her eyes. But he also saw anger. That was her steel backbone showing and it was so damn attractive. Luc knew he needed a sub in the bedroom, however, in the rest of life he wanted a woman who could stand on her own two feet. One who allowed herself to be cared for with grace and humility when the occasion called for it rather than one who needed to be taken care of 24/7. A partner.

"L…let me see the picture of it."

"I'm not so sure that's a good idea," Luc said as he palmed her face, rubbing his thumb back and forth across her jawline.

"Please don't try to protect me from this. It's my life. I need to know."

His beautiful girl was a strong woman. But she shouldn't have to deal with this shit. Luc relented at the sight of the determined look in her eyes. He pulled up the picture on his phone and passed it to her. Her eyes flared, and her hand covered her mouth as she shook her head.

"No! Not Merlot! Oh, Luc. I'm so sorry this has now involved your family. It's all my fault." Sobs came freely as she buried her face in her hands.

"This is not your fault. Gryff will get this asshole behind bars where he can't threaten or hurt anyone again."

Avery pulled away with a start, her spine stiff.

"Oh my God. I have to get to Cassie. What if they go after her? Luc, I have to get to her."

Gryff's car barreled around the corner and down the driveway toward them. Luc pulled up to where Gryff stopped. Before he could put the car in park, Avery opened her door and was mid-stride toward Gryff. What was that churning in his gut? Why would the vision of Avery practically leaping into his buddy's arms for consolation get to him? Pretending he wasn't jealous was more of a challenge than he thought. It must have been written all over his face. Gryff saw it and silently told him to stand down.

"Shhh. He's getting bolder. It means he's about to make a

mistake, and then we'll have him," Gryff reassured Avery, stroking up and down her back as she sobbed in his arms.

Luc needed to keep his shit together. Avery needed him too. He walked toward the two friends and quietly caressed Avery`s arm. Gryff nodded with approval.

"This fucker is seriously pissing me off, Gryff. We need to get his ass behind bars now."

A very was grateful for her steadfast friendship with Gryff, but she was utterly and completely done with the victim role. She allowed herself to cry in Gryff's arms. Just to get it out of her system. Now she was done.

As she lifted her weary head from Gryff's solid chest she was struck by the magnificent sunrise casting an ethereal glow over Sky Hill's vineyards. When she was up this early it was for her morning yoga and meditation routine. Rarely had she simply stopped to soak in the sheer beauty of this time of day, particularly this close to such a pristine vineyard. She spun to face the sun's fortifying rays, drinking in the energy as they warmed her face.

The chaotic white noise of fear clanging in her head dulled to a manageable roar and her breath was no longer shallow and labored. She absorbed the gold and amber hues of sunlight washing over the vines and felt renewed. Her inner warrior goddess was finally waking up from her much-too-long slumber.

She took one last fortifying deep breath, blew it out, and looked to Gryff then to Luc, and with an emphatic wave of her arms marked her line in the proverbial sand.

"I'm done. I'm so frikin' done letting this asshole run my life with fear. He did it for too long when we were married and as soon as he got out of jail he started up again. Well, Mister Thinks-he's-the-man-Winters, I'm *not* playing your mind games anymore. Boys, I'm taking my life back. To hell with Cal Winters."

The look of pride shining in both men's eyes fueled her adrenaline rush even higher than it already was from her impassioned little speech. But just as quickly, that pride morphed into concern, even fear. She caught Luc and Gryff exchanging knowing glances — silent communication that used to bug her when they were kids, now it kind of intrigued her — to a point.

"Cut it out, you guys. I'm standing right here. If you have something to say, out with it."

"OK, OK. We're proud of you for standing your ground," Luc said with both his hands up in a sign of surrender.

"But?"

Gryff jumped in. "But, it's clear whoever's trying to scare you is getting bolder. This latest incident with Merlot is a step up. Until now, no one was hurt. The previous messages were designed to catch you off guard, shake you up, but not hurt you. Also, we're not completely convinced it's actually your asshole of an ex-husband who's trying to scare you."

She looked from Gryff to Luc with newfound concern and more questions. "If not Cal, then who would want to scare me and hurt Merlot? I can`t imagine anyone other than him doing this."

"That's the million-dollar question. The fact remains, Avery, we don't have any proof one way or the other it's Cal. It seems a little too convenient to pin this all on him. We need to be open to all possibilities."

Avery's shoulders sagged, and she let out a sigh that sounded like she was about to give up. Luc's big hands gripped her shoulders and gave a gentle shake.

"Come on now, we're not giving up and neither should you. Where's that determined woman who stood in front of us two minutes ago proclaiming she was done with fear running her life?"

She straightened her spine, threw her shoulders back, lifted her chin, and flashed Luc her best warrior goddess glare.

The corner of Luc's sultry mouth curled up. "She's baaaack."

Gryff nodded with approval. "That's our girl."

"So," Avery challenged them both, "what's the plan?"

20

L uc followed Avery back to her place once the forensics team released her car. Of course, she insisted she didn't need a babysitter, but both he and Gryff would not let her go home alone. In fact, going forward, she and Cassie would have a shadow with them at all times. In the fifteen-minute drive between Sky Hill and Avery's home, Luc and Gryff hammered out the plan over the phone. Gryff headed back to his office to call in a few favors from a couple of buddies on the force, as well as his brothers. Now it was up to Luc to convince Avery to accept what they had arranged.

He pulled into Avery's driveway behind her car, noting the unmarked police car at the curb. Reaching for his Glock in the glovebox, Luc checked the magazine and safety, shoved extra ammo in his pocket and jumped to open Avery's door before she had a chance to unbuckle her seatbelt.

"Seriously, Luc? Is the gun necessary? You're freaking me out, here."

"Yes."

Master Luc was the personification of cool and calm. He

called upon his years of martial arts training to regulate his breath, heart rate, and focus while his eyes methodically scanned the area. He also used his body to shield her from the street with his larger frame as they walked up the front steps. At the front door, Luc held out his hand like he had the first night he brought her home. She shook her head, her eyebrows pinched together, and her lips pursed but handed over her keys anyway. *So far so good.* He wasn't sure if it was the submissive responding to the Dom or that she was too exhausted to argue. Either way, he'd work with it. The possibility that she felt the need to please him, even in the fallout of another scare, had his cock twitching.

Luc slipped the key into the deadbolt and turned, the expected *thunk* absent. With his gun at the ready he pushed Avery aside where she would be shielded by the brick wall of the house, then opened the front door.

"Adam! It's Luc. We're here."

"We're clear. You can come in," Detective Adam Ricci, Gryff's partner, responded from inside the house.

Avery burst past both men. She was a woman on a mission. Luc tucked his gun into the back waistband of his jeans and followed his little spitfire into her home. If he wasn't so unsettled about these messages, he would have had a good chuckle at her attitude.

"Look, you guys," she glared at them both, hands on her hips, "I appreciate you taking all these extra precautions, but come on. I don't want us to feel like prisoners in our own home. Can we dial back the macho shit a bit? Please?"

A dark, possessive growl initiated in his stomach and invaded his heart. This gutsy, gorgeous woman didn't deserve to be terrorized like this. Priority number one was Avery's and Cassie's safety. She may not like the plan he and Gryff devised, but she would comply. The only question that remained — would it be Luc, the Man, or Luc, the Master, she obeyed?

Soft, morning light streaming through the blinds illuminated her face. Her eyes were sullen, the determination he saw back in the winery parking lot had faded. The tough chick act was wearing thin, though he gave her top marks for the valiant effort.

His long legs crossed the floor in two strides to where she stood. A fine tremble had enveloped her entire body even though her obstinate scowl still marred her delicate features. The dread and resignation, now evident in her eyes, knocked the wind out of him.

"Avery," he spoke gently, rubbing his hands up and down her arms as if to force away a chill. Sliding his hands over her shoulders, one slipping down to the small of her back, the other up under the thick, golden strands at her nape, he pulled her flush against his body and tucked her head against his chest.

"I don't know what to do, Luc. I can't even walk into my own home without you making sure there's no one lurking in the shadows. What happens when you go to work?"

She pulled out of his reach and strode away from him, her arms gesturing emphatically, but not before he saw tears well up in her crystal blue eyes, threatening to spill over onto her creamy cheeks.

Lap number one.

Walls framed the central stairs leading both up and down forming a center block, typical of these older homes. Arches opened each room to the next, forming a sort of track circling the main floor. The starting gate/finish line was the foyer. Out of the gate, heading for the back turn her voice was muted. Rounding the home stretch and heading for the finish line her voice returned to full volume.

"I have to go to work too. We have lives and responsibilities. I refuse to let this asshole, whoever it is, disrupt our lives. Yet I can't shake this feeling that makes my skin crawl. It's like I'm being followed or watched. I check over my shoulder in crowds and parking lots but no one's there."

Around she went for another lap. He nodded to Adam, who took the hint and quietly let himself out.

"I'm back to checking every window and door every time I come home, go out, or even move from room to room. Cassie is supposed to be heading off to her first overnight camp this afternoon. Should I let her go? Will she be safe up there?"

Avery stopped pacing and collapsed on the sofa in the family room, tears streaming down her face, head slumping to rest on the back like the weight was too much for her to hold up. Luc perched on the coffee table in front of her, knees to knees, and placed his hands on her thighs, giving them a squeeze.

"Avery." No response. "Avery." This time it was Master Luc who spoke.

Her head popped up, trepidation, alarm, confusion, then anger skating across her gaze. Understandable given what she'd been through. The anger lingered. *Good.*

"Gryff is working on a plan right now. He and I mapped it out on the drive over here."

Her eyes went wide. "What? You two can't plan our lives."

"Avery, you're not alone. Gryff and I weren't there to protect you from Winters when you were married to the prick. But we sure as hell are here now, and no one is going to hurt you or Cassie again. Do you hear me?"

"But we don't know if it's Cal sending these messages or who hurt Merlot. Oh God, poor Merlot. I'm so thankful he'll be OK. It's all my fault he was poisoned. You have to go, Luc. Whoever is doing this knows of our connection." Avery bolted to her feet and marched to the front door. "Leave. Protect your family. Run Sky Hill and forget about me. You don't need this headache."

Gryff had warned him to take a soft approach, that Avery would resent feeling steamrolled. It pissed Luc off his friend knew more about handling his beautiful girl than he did. But, Gryff hadn't seen how gorgeous she looked with her hands latched onto the lighting sconce the night of the awards when she came all over his tongue. He hadn't seen how she took control last night when they found Merlot in the ditch. He hadn't seen how anger fueled her hunger for Master Luc despite the shit that just came out of her mouth. Master Luc understood how to make this exquisite sub embrace their plan, embrace their protection, and embrace her submission. To him.

Luc pointed to the floor by the sofa in front of where he stood and commanded, "Kneel, sub."

Every muscle in Avery's body jerked to attention. Her eyes flew open wide then shuttered closed just as fast. Deliberation, fast and furious, took place inside her head. Man, what he wouldn't give to be in the gallery listening to those arguments. He took a breath and waited, his eyes never leaving her. She needed to come to him on her own. Hell, he needed her to accept his protection.

A full two minutes he watched and waited. He would have stood there into next week if that was what she needed. Soft padding of her feet over the carpet was the only sound she made. With her eyes downcast, Avery made her way to the spot where Luc had pointed and dropped to her knees. Her technique wasn't smooth nor was her position exactly what he liked, but he'd take it any way she gave it, for now.

Luc placed his hand on the top of her head. "Thank you, beautiful girl. I know how difficult that was for you. You need to know that I will cherish your gift. You are a remarkably strong woman. I promise to respect that strength and provide the environment for it to thrive. Will you do me the honor of accepting my protection until the threat against you and Cassie has been eliminated?"

One step at a time.

He knew how to help protect her, how to solve any legal woes, even knew how to finesse her with wine, gourmet food, and sex. What he didn't know how to do was help her feel whole again. That was something he couldn't command. Would his brand of Dominance give her a safe place where she could feel rooted, confident, and worthy of being loved? Could he love her enough to give her that gift of freedom to be herself? Love? Luc was pleasantly surprised that the word didn't have him running for the hills. There was no doubt what he was feeling for Avery was love blooming in his soul. And it felt right.

Need alone dropped her to her knees at Luc's feet. It didn't require arduous list-making of pros and cons. Well, she'd started on the pros but gave up when she felt moisture gathering in her folds. Maybe it was time to start listening to her instincts again.

There was an inexplicable dialogue between them that existed beyond the spoken word. Call it pheromones, lust, loneliness, maybe even comfort or familiarity. Luc and Avery. Man and woman. Dominant and submissive.

Apprehension melted into the nether with Luc's touch. She felt safe with him. Not only would he never hurt her, he was willing to stand beside her and protect her. And what was even more remarkable was how he had Cassie's safety in mind too. She fell a little in love with him in that moment.

Avery looked up into his expressive, molten chocolate eyes and felt a sense of calm wash over her frazzled nerves. With that calm came heat and hunger. The bulge in the front of Luc's jeans confirmed the want she saw in his eyes, but there was more. There was tenderness coming from somewhere deep inside. Could it be from his heart?

She'd be crazy to allow herself to go there. No way would Luc want to become entangled in her crap. Focus on today. Get Cassie off to camp and put a plan in place to take care of Cal once and for all. Then, maybe, she could entertain luscious daydreams about Mr. Christianson. Her body shuddered as she imagined his finely hewn body hovering over her, commanding her, ravishing her and pleasuring her beyond her wildest fantasies. If previous encounters were any indication of what could lie ahead...good thing she was already on her knees, otherwise she'd have been flat on her ass from the full-body swoon that rolled over her.

Luc kneeled in front of her — thigh to thigh, hip to hip, chest to chest. He peppered gentle kisses on her forehead, down one side of her face, under her jaw and back up the other side. So delicate. Even reverential. Avery felt cherished for the first time in her life. Luc leaned back and captured her gaze.

"I see the heat in your eyes, beautiful girl. I feel it too. There's nothing more I would love to do at this moment than turn you over on your hands and knees, ass in the air, and bury my cock so deep inside you, thoughts of any other man in your life will become non-existent. Just you and me."

"Please, Luc," she gasped. The English major and writer was without words.

"Mmm. Your body is on board with that idea," Luc said as he traced his fingers along Avery's pulsating carotid artery. Not that her shallow pants hid her cravings any better.

Luc's explicit dirty talk also prompted her now self-deter-

186 | HÉLÈNE SOPER

mined body to show a dash of bashfulness by making her chest and cheeks a canvas for all the shades of crimson in a warm Niagara sunset. She was going to combust as sure as the sun continued to burn bright.

Luc chuckled as Avery's blush climbed to the tips of her ears.

"My body is completely on board, too. But first, we need to talk about how our plan to keep you and Cassie safe is going to go."

Avery's brain wanted to rebel against leaving her and Cassie's fate in someone else's hands. She'd fought hard to become an independent woman and mother again. She didn't need anyone to protect her or make plans for her future. No way was she going to just give up and go along with Gryff and Luc's plan. For. Get. It. Unfortunately, she couldn't muster the indignity required to be pissed off. Master Luc rendered her internal deny-entry-at-all-costs warrior goddess as effective as a licky-face puppy would be as a guard dog.

Luc leaned back against the couch, pulling her with him and nestling her between his legs on the floor. His nose brushed against the tender spot behind her ear and whispered, "I've got you, little one. Trust me and Gryff to keep you and your precious daughter safe. Can you do that?"

This was Luc, her friend, Gryff's best friend. She trusted Gryff with her and Cassie's safety. And apparently, Luc was also part of that security plan. They knew more about how to keep them safe than she did. History had shown that, and it was coming back to bite her in living color. History was a bitch. Avery let out a long sigh, hopeful she'd banished the constant trepidation about losing herself again.

"I know you and Gryff mean well and are trying to do the right thing. I'm just having a hard time with decisions being made about my life, about my daughter's life, without my input. I've lived that hell, and I refuse to be sucked back in."

That's what Cal had done. Looking back, it was obvious. He'd systematically isolated her from her friends, family, and eventually work for what he had called "her well-being." He'd decided what she would wear, what they would eat, what television shows and movies were "appropriate" for her to watch. Without a support system, Cal's insidious maneuvers set up the perfect environment for their marriage to devolve into master and slave. Not the consensual power exchange Marlowe and Gryff described to her. Cal fed off her insecurities in order to mask his own. It was a complete power shift. She was left with none and Cal held it all, wielding it with malice. No safewords allowed.

"That's fair. Why don't you hear what we propose? If something doesn't sit well with you or doesn't work with your schedule, we can discuss it and come up with an alternative. OK with you?"

Avery pulled away from his comforting embrace, so she could see his face. Tiny lines at the corners of his eyes creased with his gentle smile. His gaze was steady, solid, and sure. There was no doubt it was Master Luc speaking with her, but this beautiful, intelligent, intense man didn't use his power to scare her, rather, he openly shared it with her. She could do this.

"OK," Avery sighed, "what have you two come up with?"

Luc's phone buzzed with a text. He showed her the screen — it was from Gryff. Luc quickly read the message and nodded as if he was pleased with what Gryff wrote.

"First, Gryff's brother Zach is en route to Cassie's camp ahead of her bus. Gryff contacted the camp and explained the situation to the director. The scheduled martial arts instructor was a friend of Zach's, so they switched places. Zach will be teaching the classes at the camp, so he can be near Cassie the whole time

188 | HÉLÈNE SOPER

she's away. One of Gryff's buddies on the force will follow the bus up to the camp to make sure Cassie arrives safe and sound. Second, Gryff is coming by to check on a few things here and I'm heading to the office. Then I'm going to grab some of my stuff and I will be back. I'm bringing dinner and I'm staying the night. You are not going to be alone until this sonofabitch is behind bars. In the morning, Gryff will escort you to the office. He's also going to have a word with the security guys at the paper to let them in on what's going on. So far so good?"

Avery was overwhelmed. Grateful. Someone would be with her 24/7 while Cassie was safely ensconced in her camp in Algonquin Park with Zach, oblivious to everything happening at home. Tears trickled down her cheeks as she resigned herself to the plan. Part of her was enormously relieved she wouldn't be facing this nightmare alone. Another part of her was pissed she had to even contemplate these kinds of security measures. Hadn't she lived through enough already? And what about her darling angel? She was growing up to be a vibrant little girl. She would do anything to wipe away the past so her daughter could live without any of this crap hanging over her head. She was too young to remember the details of that horrible night when they left Cal for good, and the violence that preceded it. She was old enough now to have this latest episode leave ugly scars. Avery needed to put aside her own misgivings about surrounding her little family with these big men and their guns. All she could do was hope whoever this bastard was would show his face soon so they could catch him and finally close this chapter of her life.

"I'm with you and thank you. But, honestly, do we need this level of security?" Her voice was small and hopeful this was overkill.

"Avery, we know what Cal is capable of. We're not sure this is his work, but I'm not prepared to risk you or Cassie being hurt ever again. Think of it this way…you have cops and self-defense experts in your life now. Let us do this for you. It would make us feel a whole lot better knowing we took the steps necessary to protect you and Cassie. We weren't able to last time. We also want to make sure that when he strikes again, and make no mistake he will, we will be there to catch the asshole. Are you with us?"

"Um, yeah. I…I need to finish getting Cassie's stuff ready," Avery said as she jumped to her feet, wiping her face with the heels of her hands. "My mom is coming by to pick up her gear then take her to meet the camp bus. Do you want some coffee? I can put some on before I go upstairs."

Luc held onto her hand, stopping her escape to the kitchen. He spun her back to face him and pinned their bodies together, foreheads tenderly touching, gazes glued to each other.

"Hold on. Either you're afraid of me or you're hiding something from me. I don't care for either scenario. I would much prefer the truth, little one. Talk to me."

"Oh, of course I'm not afraid of you, Luc. I just need to get moving so Cassie's not late for the bus."

It was important he believed this to be true. And it was. But, she didn't want to scare him away by revealing what was deepening in her heart. Omission wasn't lying, right?

Luc had made it perfectly clear he wasn't a celibate monk over the past five years. Sex was just sex. No strings. No feelings. He hadn't had a serious relationship since his wife and daughter were killed. His encounters with women had been D/s scenes.

Last night was a revelation into his psyche. He would always love his wife, that was understandable. But, could he fall in love again? More importantly did Avery want to risk her heart only to have it smashed to dust when he figured out he couldn't or wouldn't open his heart to her? So why did she feel more than a casual vibe coming from him? It felt more like possession. And she liked it. A lot.

She needed some distance. She also craved Luc. Her childhood crush had blossomed into full-on, completely adult, raging need and quite possibly head-over-heels love. What was a girl to do? What was a girl who wore her emotions on her sleeve and couldn't lie to save her life to do? Deflect to protect.

"Let's just say, it's been a little overwhelming being me lately."

Luc chuckled. "That's an understatement. How about I go make the coffee while you get started upstairs?"

Crisis averted. For the moment, anyway.

"Sounds good. The coffee and filters are in the cupboard above the coffee maker."

As she finished the instructions and placed her foot on the first stair, Luc gripped her wrist and pulled her back in front of him. She couldn't look up at his face, afraid to see disappointment in his eyes. She sighed and lowered her eyes to the sliver of carpet separating their feet.

"Little one," Luc began, his voice carrying censure and compassion in equal measure, "lying to me is not acceptable. However, I'm going to give you a pass because today has been an emotional roller coaster, and I don't want to contribute to that maelstrom. But make no mistake, in the future, lying or avoiding communicating with me will be cause for punishment. Do I make myself clear?"

Punishment? What the hell did that mean? A shiver lit a blaze of fire up Avery's spine as she bit the corner of her lower lip, color blooming in her cheeks.

"Interesting. It seems my beautiful girl is turned on by the mere thought of punishment. I'll file that away for future reference."

Shit. No hiding her arousal from Master Luc. Why in the hell would the potential of being slapped on her ass or denied orgasm be so hot? Because it would be Luc administering the discipline he felt appropriate. Not to mention the screaming, body melting orgasm that would surely follow.

And *my* beautiful girl? Interesting indeed.

Luc and Avery's story doesn't end here. Their HEA comes in *Show Me How to Live: Part 2*, but not without a shocking twist that will leave you breathless.

Stay up-to-date with book releases, cover reveals, and exclusive content for newsletter subscribers and our Facebook reader group. Click the links below to join us.

Social links

Website: **HeleneSoper.com**
Newsletter: **HeleneSoper.com**
Facebook: **HeleneSoperAuthor**
Twitter: **@Helene_Soper**

ACKNOWLEDGMENTS

Thank You

It's said it takes a village to raise a child. This book has taken four years and a small city to finally come to life. There are so many wonderful people who have encouraged and inspired me throughout this journey to become an author. Please forgive me if I've not included you below. Just know I appreciate everything — positive and negative — you have all contributed. I've taken it all as a learning experience that I will forever cherish and hopefully become a better writer for it.

To Kim, Karma, Kathy, Laurel, Annabel, Erica, Jacki, and Becky. Thank you for your early feedback and advice as I learned about the craft of writing and the business of publishing. Your patience with my clumsy plot and endless questions was instrumental in kicking my ass to dive deep into the process and figure shit out. You know how I love a challenge. I'm truly grateful for your time and encouragement.

To my critique partner Lilith Darville. Thank you is inadequate to express my gratitude for you taking a leap of faith and asking a newbie to work with you. You convinced me I'm good enough to give this thing a go. I'm not sure I would be here today without you. Your insights into these characters have been invaluable and have shaped this story in countless ways. I can only hope I have contributed to your work in a small way. And you rock as a travel buddy!

To Judy, Sharon, and Mark. Thank you for your enthusiasm for my baby. You asked questions that challenged me to dig below the surface to polish my rough little gem. I can't wait to see what's next.

To my boys, Paul and Alex. You have supported and encouraged me all along. Your genuine desire to see me succeed at this thing of mine fills my heart. Thank you for letting me hide out in my writing cave so I could bring to life these pesky characters percolating in my brain. Fair warning — there are more clawing to get out and onto the page. I love you both more than words can say.

ALSO BY HÉLÈNE SOPER

Show Me How to Live: Part 1

A Bacchus House Novel (Book 1)

Show Me How to Live: Part 2

A Bacchus House Novel (Book 1.5)

ABOUT THE AUTHOR

Hélène Soper is a mom, wife, and Niagara Wine Country insider whose vivid imagination sometimes gets the better of her.

By day she's a marketer, and at night her creative juices get a work out conjuring plot twists designed to keep her characters from falling in love. But inevitably they do have their happily ever after because who doesn't need a good HEA in their life.

Her stories use kink as a tool for her characters to discover their true freaky natures and to forge a bond that makes even the bad guys jealous.

In her spare time, she loves sipping Niagara wine while reading a steamy romance novel with her two feline furbabies curled into her side.

Website: **HeleneSoper.com**
Newsletter: **HeleneSoper.com**
Facebook: **HeleneSoperAuthor**
Twitter: **@Helene_Soper**

Made in the USA
Middletown, DE
14 December 2018